JONNY
APPLESEED

JONNY
APPLESEED

A Novel

JOSHUA
WHITEHEAD

ARSENAL PULP PRESS
VANCOUVER

ARSENAL PULP PRESS
Suite 202 – 211 East Georgia St.
Vancouver, BC V6A 1Z6
Canada
arsenalpulp.com

The publisher gratefully acknowledges the support of the Canada Council for the Arts and the British Columbia Arts Council for its publishing program, and the Government of Canada, and the Government of British Columbia (through the Book Publishing Tax Credit Program), for its publishing activities.

This is a work of fiction. Any resemblance of characters to persons either living or deceased is purely coincidental.

Cover and title page artwork by Erin Konsmo
Cover and text design by Oliver McPartlin
Edited by Brian Lam
Printed and bound in Canada

Library and Archives Canada Cataloguing in Publication:
Whitehead, Joshua, 1989-, author
    Jonny Appleseed / Joshua Whitehead.
Issued in print and electronic formats.
ISBN 978-1-55152-725-3 (softcover).—ISBN 978-1-55152-726-0 (HTML)
    I. Title.
PS8645.H5498J66 2018   C813'.6   C2017-907218-8
                                                C2017-907219-6

For nohkômak, kisâkihitin;

& for Terri Cameron, I miss you every day.

I

I figured out that I was gay when I was eight. I liked to stay up late after everyone went to bed and watch Queer as Folk on my kokum's TV. She had a satellite and all the channels, pirated of course. At the time, my mom and I were living with my kokum because my dad had left us—I think he took Loretta Lynn a little too seriously because one day he never did come home after drinking. Queer as Folk was on at midnight; I muted the channel with the subtitles turned on so no one would hear it, and turned down the brightness so the glaring light wouldn't shine underneath their doors like the goddamn poltergeist. I loved QAF; I wanted to be one of those gay men living their fabulous lives in Pittsburgh. I wanted to live in a loft and go to gay bars and dance with cute boys and fool around in gloryholes. I wanted to work in a comic shop or a university, I wanted to be sexy and rich. I wanted that. I used to jack off to Brian Kinney's junk and pause on Justin Taylor's bare white ass to finish. To keep my kokum's brown floral couch clean, I brought my blanket and afterwards wiped myself with a tube sock. I always swallowed my breath and curled my toes tightly to avoid gasping whenever I was about to come. When I finally did, I thought, this must be what beauty feels like: my skin tight and burning, body wet as mud.

When I got a little older, I think I was fifteen, I remember watching Dan Savage and Terry Miller on the internet telling me that *it gets better*. They told me that they knew what I was going through, that they knew me. How so, I thought? You don't know me.

You know lattes and condominiums—you don't know what it's like being a brown gay boy on the rez. Hell, I'd never even seen a Starbucks and I sure as hell couldn't tell you why a small coffee is called "tall." That's also around the time when I began to collect clients like matryoshka dolls, so I suppose at least my income got better. This was of course before the photo-sharing apps and cam sites that I use now to conduct my business, but at that time, the internet was packed with people wanting to connect with other people, especially there in Peguis. We had Facebook and cellphones to keep us in the loop. I used to sext with others in chatrooms on a gaming website, Pogo. I went by the name Lucia and pretended to be a girl to flirt with other boys. Often we'd play virtual pool or checkers and just dabble in small talk. Then I'd start putting ideas of sex into their heads by playing naïve and directing the conversation toward dirty subjects. I always liked to let them think they were the ones in control. I'm a sadist like that, I guess. I may be the sexual fantasy but I'm also the one in the driver's seat. Once the image of sweaty, naked bodies got in their heads, there was no going back. Sex does strange things to people—it's like blacking out or going on cruise control. Your body knows what it wants and goes for it. This can be dangerous, as I'd learn later, but if you can manipulate the urge, you can control a person. I felt like Professor Xavier—like I was telepathic.

That was how my webcam career began, with virtual pool and cybersex. That was how I met Tias. He was my first cyber boyfriend—I was the Russian princess Lucia and he was the five-years-older-than-he-really-is Native boy who dreamed of losing his virginity.

We were quite the couple.

At the time I wasn't out, but the others at school knew I was different. They called me fag, homo, queer—all the fun stuff. But I never let it bother me. I sometimes caught both girls and boys sneaking glances at my body. I went by a hundred different names. No one outside of my family called me Jonny; everyone knew me as The Vacuum. If you'd ever known me between the ages of twelve and today, you have probably come across me as The Vacuum. A friend at school gave me that nickname when I shotgunned a can of Lucky in less than eight seconds; apparently that's the world record for NDNs. Later, I took my nickname further and would use different vacuum brands as my name; I've been Hoover, Kirby, Makita, DD (short for DirtDevil), and sometimes, especially after my mom brought me home a new shirt from her trip to Giant Tiger in the city, I would go by Dyson—when I was feeling extra fancy.

You see, I've never liked my birth name, Jonny. My parents named me after my dad, a residential school survivor, alcoholic, and would-be country star. I never heard from him again after he left. We found out later that he died in a fire on another rez. I really don't care. People don't forget those stories, you know? Random people would ask me, "Oh you're so-and-so's boy, the drunk?" And to top off the name-shaming, one summer I went to this Christian day camp called Camp Arnes. There our counselor, Stephen, would always make us sing a song before we ate our meals. It was called "Johnny Appleseed" and it went like this:

Oh, the lord is good to me
and so I thank the lord
for giving me the things I need
like the sun and the love and the family I need.
Oh, the lord is good to me, Johnny Appleseed, amen.

Sounds dandy, right? Well, it was at that same camp that I kissed my first boyfriend, Louis—a silver fox who was a camp counselor like Stephen—and as we made out in my bunk (in Red Fox Bay), one of Louis's coworkers walked in on us. Turns out Louis had this girlfriend in Quinzhee Bay and when we got caught, he got all up in arms and blamed me for coming onto him. A few hours later, everyone at the camp heard about the incident and started calling me Jonny Rottenseed. Then lo and behold, during our pre-meal prayer, no one had their eyes closed or their heads bowed; they were all glaring at me and whispering to each other with disgust and paranoia on their faces. Even at the age of ten, an NDN can become a gay predator, apparently. And what does that even mean? Can't a boy have a sex drive? Is it such a crime if I want to touch my body and want it be touched? It's mine, annit?

When I got back to the rez, I did some research about my namesake at our shoddy little makeshift library. There was no Dewey Decimal system there; books were scattered in piles that were designated as Pile A (the Cosmos), Pile B (Peguis Fishermen yearbooks), and Pile C (random shit)—so it made being a Nancy Drew especially difficult. It turns out that Johnny Appleseed is some American folk legend who became famous by planting apple trees in West Virginia. I didn't understand why we'd sung about him at camp—I wanted to know about Louis Riel, Chief Peguis, and Buffy St. Marie, but instead we were honouring some white man throwing apple seeds in frontier America. Apparently he was this moral martyr figure who remained a virgin in exchange for the promise of two wives in heaven. Oh, and he loved animals, and I heard he saved some horse by hand-feeding him blades of grass, Walt Whitman-style. I would bet my left nut that he was a slave owner too and planted his apple seeds on Treaty territory. All I know is this: apples are crazy expensive on the rez and they had now become bad things in my head.

My stepdad Roger called me an apple when I told him I wanted to leave the rez.

"You're red on the outside," he said, "and white on the inside."

II

When I first left the rez and moved to Winnipeg, I used Grindr and Rez Fox to find friends—with benefits, of course. My apartment was full of whiteness—white lights, walls, ceiling, even toilet. The toilet we had on the rez was so old it had turned a mocha-ombre colour, and the lid, which broke when I was a kid, was only replaced with my cousin's after he died in a snowmobile accident. My mom spruced it up by adding a fluffy red cover she bought from Wal-Mart. "I saw it in the Marlborough once," she said, "thought it looked right fancy." An NDN bathroom is a star-blanket of colours collected from garage sales, hand-me-downs, and Goodwills. Once, back when I was a kid, I was at a family barbecue scarfing down my kokum's rainbow peanut butter marshmallow squares, and my older cousins snuck me a few shots of Bacardi 151—it burned all the way down. Eleven years old and drunk in the early afternoon, I ran to my kokum's bathroom and threw up a confetti of colours into her toilet. The bowl was full of rum and peanut butter and chewed-up marshmallows. When I was done, I flushed the toilet, but the damn thing wouldn't flush. In a panic, I opened the back of the toilet and scooped up the barf with my hands and deposited it into the tank. A few days later, my uncle told us over tea and bannock that "some drunk jackass puked in the tank and god-damn mold started growing back there." I felt a little proud that I had been ordained into that world, but my face reddened at the same time.

On Grindr I found a pool of men in Winnipeg all with funny names like Fotohomo and Nudedude and I thought, who are these Dr Seuss wannabes? There were shirtless dudes left and right and within minutes I had collected a storybook of dick-pics. I thought that these boys could learn a thing or two from my artistic selfies, they're a hell of a lot more than peach and eggplant emojis. All their profiles said "looking to chat" and "please be respectable" and I wondered, what does respect have to do with hooking up?

The first time I ever hooked up with a guy, we were at my friend's house party on the rez. He was a tall white kid who came with his NDN friend who had got him in the door and was acting as his go-between, otherwise the rowdy guys would have probably kicked his ass. He came in a shirt and tie and told everyone he was studying psychology in school. His friend gravitated toward one of the rez girls and left him alone sitting sheepishly in a corner, his eyes darting back and forth like a security guard. His fingers were long and bony, skeletal almost, and his hair was slicked back and patchy in areas. I thought about telling him that bear grease would fix him right up, but I could tell from his thin, twinky physique that he'd shy away from anything with fat in it. He was seated quietly, his body folded into itself, his elbows glued to his sides, taking sips from his red wine as he surveyed the room. Stupid, I thought, bringing wine to a house party—it was a badge that screamed, "I'm not from here." I watched him from afar while my friend Tasha sized him up too. "He's right cute, eh?" she said. "I'm gonna snag him later." *You're stupider than you look, Tasha, that guy's gay as hell.* His foot was jiggling nervously and I thought it looked like a fishtail. I felt bad for the guy so I grabbed a can of Coors Light and sat down across from him.

"For starters, you might want to ditch your wine and drink this," I said as I cracked open the lid. "And for godsakes, take that damn tie off."

He looked at me quizzically for a second, his eyes glazing over with that strange hunger we both shared. He unclasped those bony fingers of his and smiled at me. His teeth were pink with wine stains and he had a slight red ring around his lips. How the fuck he did that was beyond me, did he place the whole of the glass around his mouth and lick the wine like a cat? I took it as a sign from Manito that this man loved rimming.

"Thank you," he said. "This wine is giving me a stomach ache."

"You want some Pepto?"

"Oh, no thank you, I try not to take medicine on account of the superbugs, you know? I don't want to develop immunity."

"Sure thing, bud," I said, "because you're not knocking back wine like it's medicine."

He laughed and I rolled my eyes—I sure as hell wasn't going to offer him bear root tea as an alternative.

"Where you from?" I asked.

"Kitchener."

"Oh yeah, that near the capital?"

"Not really, but it's a few hours by car."

"You going to take me some time, er what?" I joked.

"Well, I mean, yeah, if you're ever in the area, hit me up."

That was when I knew I had him—I could see that just talk of the capital gave him a hard-on. He told me that he was an undergraduate at McMaster. He started talking about his courses and told me something about the bystander effect.

"It's like this study where researchers set up an emergency in a controlled setting and have paid actors simply walk by and offer no help," he said.

"So, like, what's the point?"

"To analyze how crowds of people react to emergency situations—so those paid actors walk by and their response becomes infective to others around them, creating the bystander effect."

This hypothesis didn't seem too revolutionary to me—clearly he had never set foot in Winnipeg's North End. But I liked how animated he got when he talked, how his whole body seemed to curl toward me like a cedar branch. I liked how he moved his mouth around words, as if every word he said began with an 'O' and his mouth became one great 'O' and his breathing took on the rhythm of panting; his lips were wet with spit and if you looked sideways, his dimples looked like ass cheeks. I wanted to open him up, spread apart his skin, and crawl inside his body so I could pretend that I knew fancy phrases like dendrite, placebo, and law of effect—I didn't know that law but I had a few memorized by then, and each one required you to have memorized your treaty number. When he said "neocortex," I wondered if that was the part of the brain I was using to record him. The only cortex I knew was from *Crash Bandicoot*—maybe we were talking about that now?

As he kept drawling on, I touched his knee with mine. He continued talking methodically, but I could feel him press his knee back, then slowly push my legs apart like we were both riding bareback on a horse. As I turned my gaze from his mouth to his knee, I could see the outline of his dick resting tightly on his leg beneath his jeans like a steak waiting to be fried up. He caught my gaze; his eyes were bloodshot now from the haze of cigarette smoke. Suddenly I got scared. His body no longer read timid and his red eyes reminded me of the stories of the wendigo my kokum used to tell me when I was bad.

He got up and motioned to me to follow. We made our way through a group of Natives who were huddled together near the door. There was always a group of them there, smoking up a storm, and acting like the goddamn NDN police: "Who are you?" "Where you from?" "Who you know?"—you may as well bring your passport and a list of your biological attributes with you if you want to get into a rez party. He went down the stairs as if he knew where he was going, and I descended too, a few paces behind. He ducked into the laundry room in the back corner of the basement, and I followed. The cement floor was bumpy and uneven, but it was refreshingly cool on the soles of my feet. He lit a smoke and stood before me, barely lit by the glow of his cigarette. There was no door to the room, only a bed sheet that marked it off, and a bunch of dirty clothes, a lot of them for a baby and some for a little kid. He pushed them all into a single pile and sat down against it, unbuttoning his shirt. His chest was a tundra save for the few tendrils of dark hair. I moved toward him and knelt in front of him, putting my nose against his before his lips reached for mine. He lifted my shirt and my belly was bare against the dark. His fingers traced their way down the trail of my pubic hair, and his index finger met the hollow of my pelvis.

"What if someone walks in?" I said, stopping him. My body was slippery with sweat and I was embarrassed—I didn't want to have sex feeling like a pickerel.

"No one's going to come down here," he replied cockily. *How the fuck you know*, I thought, *you've never even been here before.*

"Lots of people snag here, hell, that's what that there is for." I lip pointed toward the mattress in the corner.

He sighed and got up. He pulled the mattress over to the door to block it.

"Here, now if anyone comes in at least we'll have a few minutes to throw something on before they can move this," he said. He stood over me, his tall figure barely visible as my eyes adjusted to the dark. The floor was cold but his large hands were like coals over me. They seemed bigger now, wide enough to papoose me. He unbuckled his fly and let loose a hard flap of skin that pointed back up at him. He pulled my legs and slid me down while he maneuvered his hip against my ear and with a slight twirl I was tasting him. The roux of his juice—the leaking of white ectoplasm swishing in my mouth. I wanted this but didn't know what to do with it. I always wondered how he performed that magic, how he shapeshifted his body in the dark, how his edges poked me but never cut me, how he fit into me like a nipple fits into a baby's mouth, how I could read him upside down. His transforming body wrapped around me, blanketed me, made me sweat ceremonially. When he came, he grunted like a sow and his body clamped down on me like a snout.

Sex has always had a magic, an ability to awaken things in me that have died. After we wiped each other off, he buttoned up his jeans and left. I cried. My skin was warm and scratched raw. *Maskwa*, I thought, *I travel with my tongue just to meet you.*

The funny thing about Grindr is that it's full of treaty chasers. They'll fetishize the hell out of you if you tell them you're a real NDN wolf-boy, that you got arrows pointing at their faces and cocks. But I was a professional—work smart, not hard. I used the collage that I had made of dick-pics to help me gather clients. At least Grindr had a category called "Native American" which did a lot of leg work for me. "You're Indian, eh," someone would message me, and I'd reply, "Yeah, wanna see?" and link them to my websites. It was easy as pie—everyone on that damned app was obsessed with New Age shit like van-folk-Kerouacs playing gypsy in Canada and hipster shamans who collect crystals and geodes looking for an NDN to solidify their sorcery. "Want a stamp of validation? Here's my website!"

I'd get solicited for excursions from men saying things like, "Let's go on rad adventures to mystical forests and take a swim through the galaxy." The only mysticism I knew was on the backroads of the rez, like when you came face to face with a coyote who clears the path of birds with her howl, or a fox that appears in the same spot on the road every damn night just to look at you. And I always got a tickle out of how you could anthropomorphize yourself within the gay animal kingdom: "bear," "otter," "wolf," "fox," "cubs." If only these gays knew how powerful Mistahimaskwa could really be.

To be a gay bear, you need to be husky, hairy, and super masc, but when I picked a tribe name on Grindr, I chose bear since it was my clan. When men looked at my profile and saw my fierce jawline, they'd write, "You're a twink, not a bear"; *funny*, I'd think, *neither are you.* When I'd correct them, they'd get annoyed and tell me not to get so butt-hurt, with a dumbfounded obliviousness; truth be told, if anal sex is hurting that much, well, honey, you're doing it wrong. And I always had a good laugh at the ol' Creator for being so mischievous as to put the male g-spot in the anus. I read once that Anishinaabe and the Algonquins translate to "beings made out of nothing" and that we were created by the breath of gitchi Manito. I used to think that meant I had no body, so I learned how to make love as a feral a long time ago—the pow wows taught me how, they sang the skin back onto my bones.

III

Nobody prepares you for the sting when you're about to leave home. All my life I wanted to leave the rez—and every time I was about to, I stopped myself. It hurt. Leaving hurts. It's not glamorous like Julia Roberts makes it seem. I can't *eat* anything other than fried bologna or Klik for breakfast; I can't *pray* to a God I'm afraid of; and believe it or not, even in the twenty-first century, two brown boys can't fall in *love* on the rez. Sorry, Julia, your rah-rah-we're-all-the-same walk-through didn't work for me. I'm still me: a brown-skinned boy who loves the X-Men and Jake Bass.

One fact I'd learn is that leaving always hurts—home isn't a space, it's a feeling. You have to feel home and to feel it, you have to sense it: smell it, taste it, hear it. And it isn't always comfortable—at least, not an NDN home. In fact, quite often, it's uncomfortable. But it's home because the bannock is still browning in the oven and your kokum is still making tea and eating Arrowroot biscuits. It's home because it has to be—routine satiates these pangs. And, given time, it becomes mobile—you can take those rituals with you, uproot your home as if it were a flower. Yeah, maybe home is like a flower, a sunflower whose big bright head follows the sun; or maybe that's too fancy a metaphor for NDNs? Maybe we're more like dandelions, a weed that's a pest in the yard but pretty to look at. Yeah, an NDN home is like a dandelion: pretty but disposable, and imbued with a million little seeds that dissolve into wishes for little white hands that pluck.

My home is full of hope and ghosts.

IV

At the entrance to my rez there used to be this man who'd sit in a lawn chair and wave at everyone arriving. We called him "Smiling Steven," but I always called him the hostess-with-the-mostess. He's not there anymore—he's gone, like so many others. This rez is like a haunted house now. In my mind I'm there, and I look up at the empty sky that's glazed with stars that look too much like sugar. The land is barren save for the howling-talk of rez dogs and sometimes coyotes. The spring water puddles around the rez like a blanket— the muggy fog a polluted haze that reminds me of Venus, even the air hurts us now. I wonder if my uncles are still out looking for sasquatch, wonder if aliens are looking down at us and saying "I told ya so" over there from Jackhead where the NDNs all say the military stole a UFO, wonder if my kokum still remembers how to cook rice pudding. I wonder how Tias is doing, ask the Creator to exorcise his pain so he never gifts it to his children, never re-gifts it to himself.

I look at the nothingness, at the wasteland of filth, a holy hell if there was one. I look at you and feel the tears welling up. I want to ask you if you're still here listening, want to ask if you've disap-peared too? They always said our fate was to disappear and here I am thinking by god, we've mastered the art of dissolution. "Hey you," I yell into the abyss, "are you even here anymore?" And I guess the excitement and the dry harsh wind gives me a nosebleed—I feel like Elle from *Stranger Things* holding weights much too heavy for little girly-boys. I feel the blood seeping from my nose, speaking a forgotten Cree that repeats: *freeme, freeme, freeme.*

These days I find myself far too often talking with myself. The wind ruffles my hair; I hold my palms out to the darkness and wait for someone to take me.

V

The skies are grey these days and I got used to telling myself that it's just my kokum having a great smudge in Saskatoon and that this smoke, which smells of cedar and ash, is her medicine floating across the border. But it hangs in my living room and seeps into my drapes, clings to my skin, and nestles itself deep inside the threads of my star blanket—which now lies in the shape of a body since gone. My apartment is a room of scents that stick to the walls: the smoke from a Saskatchewan forest fire, kush, the too-sweet smell of browning bananas, the pungent stink of sex. I start my mornings like this: I wake up, take a piss, warm up last night's coffee, and open the rickety window in my bathroom where I usually do my smoking, since my building is a no-smoking zone. I butt them out in an old Diet Pepsi can that has seen better days. There isn't much to see beyond my bathroom window but the grey-grit of the Odeon's bricks, a rusting fire escape, and a pigeon building its nest on the windowsill of an abandoned building across the alley. Every morning we meet here: me, rubbing the ash and crusty scum from my lips, and that bird neatly piling little sticks, roaches, and chicken bones on the ledge. Silly little bird, I always think, building a home in a dead place.

During the time it takes me to smoke my cigarette, we stare at each other. The pigeon cocks its head from side to side, keeping its beady eyes fixed on me, and I bob mine along to the hum of the street below. I wonder if the bird thinks the same of me, if, in its own pigeon-head, it's saying: what a silly man, making a home on the land of ghosts. We are both two queer bodies moving around in spaces that look less like a home and more like desperate lodgings; both trying to make our beds with other people's garbage. Maybe we are both dreaming of utopia, thinking that these places once used to house celebrities and other important people, and that it will imbue us with a similar vivacity? Puffing on the remnants of my cigarette, inhaling smoke more from a burning filter than tobacco, I nod at the bird and say, "I'll think you are if you think I am," and blow a cloud of smudge from my lips that smells less like the stink of ass and cock and more like the bear root that my kokum always drank. "It's magic," she'd say. "This is what woke Mistahimaskwa up."

I go and fry a couple of eggs and the heart-shaped pieces of bologna I have left, then pour myself some orange juice which only fills about a third of the glass, so I mix it with Tang and top it off with tap water—an NDN breakfast if I ever did see one. I scroll through Facebook on my phone and read lengthy monologues by people I went to high school with: so-and-so is pregnant, my cousin's cousin's boyfriend is on another bender, a rez fire, a little boy attacked by wild dogs, and a million posts about missing girls.

A beep goes off and I see a new message blinking on my screen. Someone named Hatehound has messaged me asking, "DTF?" I type back, "Who's this?" and see the three little dots telling me he's replying. He's quick, I tell myself, and I think that's a good sign for some easy cash. Quick guys don't take much work, I usually don't even have to work my way up to fingering myself, usually a few playful dick-pics will get them off and earn me a solid twenty to thirty bones; it's the slow guys you have to be careful of, they'll exhaust you and your body and still want more. Pictures and webcam shows are one thing, but let me tell you how tiring it is to create an entire world for clients that fits your body and theirs, and no one else. I can be a barely legal twink for them if they want, but that's going to cost extra—and I don't charge them for the ugly memories those fantasies dredge up. Most times, though, they only want me to play NDN. I bought some costumes a few Halloweens ago to help me: Pocasquaw and Chief Wansum Tail. Once I know what kind of body they want, I can make myself over. I can be an Apache NDN who scalps cowboys on the frontier, even though truthfully, I'm Oji-Cree.

Once, one of my clients told me I had a "red rocket" and while I moaned for him while Frank Waln rapped in the background, I continually asked him, "You want my red rocket?" Later, I looked up what "red rocket" means, and I found out that it's the dick of a dog. I thought for a second, then accepted it: I added "canine" to the list of entities I could morph into and started charging an extra few bucks per session.

Hatehound's reply showed up on my phone. "April told me about you this morning, apparently you blew his mind last night?" April? He must mean "hardck22," I think he said his name was April—I never ask for real names, but I remembered his because I laughed thinking he was joking or feeling nostalgic for spring. A part of me wanted to say, "April, eh? Yeah, and I'm fucking January Jones." Another part of me wanted to cry and confess that April was the month my kokum died. But I just laughed and I think he got mad—I wish he knew that when an NDN laughs, it's because they're applying a fresh layer of medicine on an open wound.

"Give me twenty minutes?" I replied to Hatehound. I saw the three little dots pinging on my screen and pondered who I wanted to transform into this time. I can inhabit so many personas while the client can only be one—that excites me. I have so much power when I transform—all that power over blood, veins, and nerve endings.

"Sure," he replied, and I squealed a little. I took my black velvet bodysuit from the closet. For the next thirty minutes I'd not only be Catwoman but every iteration of her, the better parts of Michelle Pfeiffer, Julie Newmar, and Anne Hathaway. When I slid the bodysuit over my calves and onto my shoulders, I watched my brown skin disappear beneath the pull of a zipper and felt so much more in control. Maybe as Catwoman I'd have the courage to ask how he could live so large and leave so little for the rest of us?

"Catwoman?" Hatehound asked after I sent him a picture. "April says you dress up as yourself, you know, with the fringe and shit? Why are you acting weird?"

I scoffed, and upped my fee to thirty dollars for the session. When he declined and sent only twenty-five to my Snapchat piggybank, I took off the cat ears and asked him: "Who are you pretending to be?"

VI

When we were kids, Tias's parents took us camping at Hecla, which was about an hour east of the rez. It was in this park, Grindstone, and full of trees, water, and white people. We took out our tents and set up in one of the lots: a little tribe of brown-skins camping in pup tents while next to us a family of three was hunkered down in an RV worth more than our house—I always wondered what the inside of those giant machines looked like. Tias and I got on our swimming trunks and headed toward the beach, which was a twenty-minute walk through the park. All around us dandelion seeds billowed through the air, twirling like ballerinas. Tias's face always seemed to soften whenever he was surrounded by nature; his usual pained expression disappeared, and the dimples in his cheeks rose like little stars.

On the beach the large waves whipped up from the wind swallowed us like crawfish. We waded into the water until it went up to our stomachs. Tias laughed and put his hand on my pouch and a finger in my navel. What a funny word, navel, but perhaps it was fitting, as my skin had pruned in the cold lake water and bubbled up like the skin of an orange—I too was full of juice. His finger continued to prod me, it felt like a leech suckling on the rump where nikâwiy cut me free. I pushed him away and then jumped on his back, laced my feet around his waist, and wrapped my arms around his shoulders, our long wet hair coming together like sweetgrass. He carried me out in the water as far as we could still stand, the shore drifting farther and farther, the water throwing our laughs back at us. When Tias was finally exhausted, he let go of me, and we stood there, looking at one another, the waves throwing us back to the shore.

"This is like *Titanic*, eh?" I said.

"Hated it, it was so long. Two fucking VHS tapes, what the—?"

"Don't be such a smart ass." I slugged him in the arm.

"Okay fine, I'm Jack, you can be Rose," he said and put his arm around my head like he was rescuing me.

"You sure?" I said. "You know I'm dink-eyed as fuck. I'd cut your damn hand off if I had to chop you free with an axe."

We continued to play in the water as our bodies became raisins—we looked like elders with tiny bodies, like NDN Benjamin Buttons. And time passed too quickly for two little Nates to measure. The sun was going down and we had drifted much too far to recount our steps. Our bodies were tired, legs drained of energy, so we linked arms and filled our bellies with air so that we could float like salmon swimming upstream. We stopped resisting the waves and let the water push us back to the shore, our shoulders and hair moussed with seafoam.

When we got back to dry land, our bodies were exhausted. I sat on the sand to catch my breath while Tias ran ahead to look for the towels we had recklessly thrown down. The sun was falling and tinted the sky lavender. Tias left a trail of prints in the sand, some disappearing from the pulse of the waves, others filling with water. I got up and followed the steady path of prints; I found him not too much farther ahead, lying exhausted in the sand. I quietly watched him for a few moments before he noticed me, his forearm glittering in the purple haze, his skin so bronzed that he melded with the sand. I sat down beside him, our naked shoulders rubbing, shaking our hair loose of the water like wet dogs, telling stories.

"You know," he began—much like he always does, the way NDNs expect you to know every story like a telepath—"I have this photo at home."

"Oh yeah?"

"Yeah. Of my sister, she's a baby—"

"You have a sister?"

"Yeah, well, *had* a sister."

"What happen? She die or something?"

"Worse. She was taken."

"You mean, like Liam Neeson kind of *Taken*?" I've never been able to handle uncomfortable situations very well. I always try to use humour to deal.

"You think this is a fucking joke?" he said, his hands rolled into fists. He kicked me and knocked me over and before I had a chance to get up, he climbed on top of me and punched me in the side of the head.

"What do you know about anything, Jonny?" Another punch. "You think because you're gay you're the only one with problems in this world?" And like that his face was pinched up with pain again, his wet ass up against my cock—I guess I got a half chub. I could tell he felt it pushing against his rear, and at first he sat there dumbfounded, didn't move, just looked down at me, his eyes like two brown worm-holes. And then he jumped off me.

"You're sick, you know that? Who the fuck gets horny from being punched?" We sat in silence for a few seconds, then both burst into laughter. "You're really something, you know that, Jonny?"

We got up and started to make our way back to the campsite—ready for the lickin we were bound to get for being so damned late. But first I wanted to collect a souvenir from the beach. As he went on ahead, I found a snail shell poking out where Tias had pushed me into the sand, and put it in my pocket. I looked down at the outline my body had made in the sand, and his right next to it; I traced the mark left from the soft hollow between his legs.

I caught up with him and we made our way back in the peppery light of the moon. The willows were shaking in the breeze, the waves now a distant world away. Tias's back was glowing from dead stars, dead light. His parents were wicked mad and sent us both to bed without any supper, called us both a "goddamn curse" for making them worry. We giggled in the tent and made shadow animals with a flashlight. His was a wolf, mine an eagle.

I never had to tell him, that was how I knew I loved him—I never had to tell him.

VII

After I had finished and cleaned myself up, I transferred the money to my bank account, typed back, "Talk soon, HH," and signed off. I lay back in my bed and traced the imprint of Tias's body with my finger. It still smelled of him, like the citrus-olive oil blend of his pomade and the robust smell of his Axe body spray, Phoenix I think he said, the blue can. It's pretty expensive, you know, especially for him, a boy still living with his rents who are, themselves, living off child-tax credits and food banks. You can get a can of Axe for a toonie though, if you ask old Peggy to pick you up a can. See, Peggy is our best NDN smuggler, she'll take a list of items you want from any department store—Wal-Mart is her favourite target—steal those items, and sell them to you for a hardcore discounted price. It benefits everyone. Momma always said that woman was the epitome of resource, that she saved up enough from pulling over to the side of the road to collect cans from ditches, got extra cash from coupon savings, and hoarded one-litre Pepsi's when they were on sale to sell at the bingo halls—said she saved up enough cash over a few years to buy her own momma a new washer and dryer. Before Uber was a thing, Peggy offered rides to people for a few bucks and if you needed a lift down to the hospital or if an Elder needed to head into town, she'd give you a ride for free so long as you threw her a few smokes and a slab or two of bannock. Momma says she's sort of the folk hero of the rez, everyone has mad respect for her. Though, these days Peggy hasn't been able to hold herself down since she got a criminal record for assaulting the social worker that scooped up her babies and now she mostly flip-flops between Winnipeg and the rez—and it works for us Nate boys who want to smell fancy for cheap. Of course, we all use each other to haggle with our own troubles—she'll save up enough for a couple king cans of Bud and pass out down Portage and us, well, we use our skills to hustle and make a few bucks. It's an endless loop. I guess that's the NDN bartering system?

And I should correct myself here, Tias isn't a hustler like me, no, he is a different kind of hustler, maybe more a prisoner than anything, but he has to live with his momma until he ages out of foster care because she needs the child-tax and he needs the roof. And between you and me? Tias is twenty, but since his original birth certificate has been sealed and rewritten, his documents say he's still seventeen. There's funding for him until he's nineteen when he'll age out and be left to his own devices. His momma is no Susan Sarandon type of mom, no, she is more like Halle Berry in *Monsters Ball*, but Tias, he's a tough kid, knows how to play the game. I like to think I helped coach him on the art of performance when he first fell in love with Lucia, the Russian princess. When he was a kid, his foster dad broke his nose on the ice because Tias asked if he was his real daddy—it's funny, you know, since his leather brown complexion didn't make any sense compared to his foster dad's porcelain skin. I guess that makes all of us NDN kids hustlers. We're cheating a system that's supposed to be doing us good.

On my bed, I nestle my body inside Tias's imprint, my knee angled into the curvature of his, my arms stretched wide, my face tilted slightly upwards. His sleeping shape looks like a ballerina. After freeing my body of its fluids, I have no reason to still be awake or to feign a smile. I want to be him too, wear his skin like a suit, cuddle it against my body as if I were a cat pressing myself against my owner's legs.

He often sleeps over and helps me prep for work. He doesn't mind, but he also says he isn't gay and I tell him me neither. I still don't think he gets what that means, even when he's inside me. At first he used to will himself to love me if I made myself more feminine, when I told him I was still Lucia. I'm fine either way, to be honest. I'm like an Etch-a-Sketch—every cell in my body is yours to define. I always tell him he can stay as long as he likes, move into my bachelor if he wants, cause lord knows I can't keep up a steady stream of seven to eight clients a day to pay this rent. He needs a lot of loving, I can feel it in the spasm of his legs when he comes, see it in the hard curl of his big toe, see it in the gnarly fingernails that his daddy cut too short after we painted them silver. Then again, I need a lot too. There are tons of unfuckable holes in me that need to be filled.

He's supposed to come over again later tonight with dinner. I think he said he had a few food stamps for Hamburger Helper, though a part of me wants to text him and say, "Let's scratch dinner because I got to make some extra cash to take off back to the rez."

See, my stepdad died this morning.

These days, I keep dreaming of Armageddon.

VIII

I have this recurring dream where I'm standing on the shore of this ocean. The sky is dark at the edges but lit by the glow of the city behind me. The water is a rich black-blue in colour and when it washes over my feet I see all sorts of things in it: mud, grass, even blood. The tide is retreating—there are dead fish, aluminum cans, and metal bolts lying in the wet sand, which shine in the glaring light of the city. But the water is not calm—it retreats only to gain momentum. And the sea foam is no precious Grecian thing—the froth bubbles black with grit and oil, burning holes into the land. As the waters retreat farther, I see a dark wave rising on the horizon. Every ounce of the ocean's strength is contained within it. And the city is panicking now—I hear air horns and blackouts and screams as loud as bombs.

And there I am—a lone brown boy naked on the precipice of the end of the world, the soles of my feet burning in the residue of an angry beach. Turtles scurry between my legs and become boulders on the sand, holding steady onto their own. I hear the doom song of orca, wolves, and bears all around me—the cacophonous cry of an animal feeling death like the texture of gauze sticky with blood and stone. A multitude of birds take flight towards the wave, carrying sticks, grass, and little rodents in their claws. They are going to fly over its crest and make a new home—somewhere over *there,* in the distant West. Suddenly a large bird, an eagle perhaps, digs its talons into my clavicles and lifts me into the sky. But it doesn't hurt, as there are grooves in my bones, grommets even, for these claws to fit. I am like a toy in an arcade machine being lifted by a claw. And the higher we go, the colder it gets, so I climb onto its back and nestle in its feathers.

The great wave is nearing and the skies are now red from a silhouetted sun, flashing lightning. Rain, hail, and winds peck at our faces, but we push on through the storm. The wave is higher than we expected. The great bird won't make it—it'll have to pierce through the crest of the wave. The winds are strong enough now that they yank out my hair and scoop out handfuls of feathers from the bird. We are weathered and worn—both of us bleeding in the sky. And I decide, if we are both to live, that I must shield the bird from the impact of the wave. So I climb higher up on its back and wrap my torso around its head, tuck my legs beneath its stout neck, pull my body tight against its, then lean in and whisper, with gentle kisses, "It's okay, it's okay."

It's okay.

Then with a great flap of its wings, we shoot through the crest of the wave. The coldness of the water stings my flesh, the pressure and force rips open my back as if it were a zipper, and the debris that churns inside the wave bruises our tired bodies. We emerge on the other side of the wave, both a bloody mess—both a sad, scalped sight flying through the sky. We ready ourselves to find a promised land on the other side with the Fur Queen and Whisky Jack waving us home, but instead we see that the water has not calmed, and there are waves as far as the eye can see. The waves are coming—they are here to take back what is rightfully theirs; we are all due—a thunderbird and Nanabush both.

IX

Tias always hated having his picture taken, but he sure loved to collect photographs. I liked to snoop through his belongings whenever I went to his house. He had one of us tucked in a collage he made for school, part of a report on Thanksgiving—how cute, I thought. In the picture we're both poking at a dead porcupine that had curled itself into a ball and looked like a dried-out dandelion. His mom took the picture and I remember how happy she was to see that porcupine dead: "Damn thing's been eating up our shed!" We all knew there was a porcupine nearby because several of the rez dogs were moping around with white quills stuck to their faces that looked like bones growing out of their mouths. I always thought porcupines were cute little animals, all grey and bunched up like a little elder. Serves people and animals right for being attacked—not everything is yours to touch. But we poked and prodded and played with that carcass for hours, pushing a little too hard on its soft belly, the stick piercing through its skin, which oozed blood.

When I told my kokum about the porcupine later, she gave me a slap upside the head and made me grab two buckets and take her to its body. When we got to the kill site, it stunk like the combination of moldy cheese and an old man's BO. But my kokum walked straight up to it, touched its soft spot, and put tobacco down for it. Then she grabbed its little paws, splayed it out like a crucifix, and began ripping the hairs out. "Bring one of them buckets over here," she said, and when I did, began tossing the clumps of hair in it. "Since you want to play with porcupines, you can help me de-quill one." I watched as she pulled the hairs out like they were weeds, making a noise like she was ripping grass out of the earth. "Gotta get these guard hairs out first, y'know?" After she was done, she took out her buck knife and started running the blade over its back. When her blade touched its skin, she flicked it downward, and the white quills started flying off. "Now you," she said, and passed me the knife, forcing me to shave its body clean from ass to neck so that we could harvest its quills. Damn thing stuck me a bunch, and cut my hand up in a few spots, but my kokum just stood over me, arms crossed. "An eye for an eye," she said. "Hope you learned your lesson." We filled up both buckets, and when we were done I carried them back home, my arms sore from scraping, while my kokum carried the porcupine which now looked like a giant chicken breast, all pimples and loose skin. "Good for eating," she said, "and quill work." At home she skinned the rest of the porcupine and cooked it in a stew, which she made me eat for three days straight, breakfast, lunch, and dinner, until we finished the pot.

"Always respect the animal," she said after the stew was all gone, "and use everything if you're going to kill one. They give their life for you, so you honour their entire body, y'hear?" I nodded, angry as all hell then, but forgiving because my kokum had a way of being easy on me even when she was punishing me. "Now, you want me to fix you a sandwich? Fry you up some eggs?"

"Heck no, gran, I'll be full for a year!"

She laughed, and I ran to put my shoes on.

"You know, Jon," she said as I made my way for the door, "porcupine was a kokum once too."

When we were kids, Tias's room was ridiculously masc: posters of the Manitoba Moose and the Winnipeg Jets, Tech Decks and Tony Hawk stickers, a nudie calendar his dad gave him. One night, I was being nosy and rummaging around in his nightstand drawer, and found a photo buried at the bottom.

"Hey Tias, what's this?"

He glanced at the photo. "Oh, that. That's ju—" He took it from my hands and stared at it intensely. "It's just an old picture."

"Is that you?"

In the picture was a little boy and an old man sitting together on the steps of a house. They're both as brown as the mud around them; the old man is chubby, his forehead crinkled like barbed wire, and his eyes deeply sunk into his head. The boy is wearing these oversized aviators and is smiling up at the man beside him, who stares straight at the camera.

"Boy you're nosy, you know that?"

I watched him study the picture again. The house looked like the ones on the rez, two-storeys, an off-green shade, and two windows on the second floor that look like eyes. We always thought our houses looked like Oscar the Grouch's—maybe they were like that everywhere? Do all rezzes look the same? Like some NDN *Sesame Street*?

"Yeah, that's me, as a little kid before I was, you know, adopted."

"That your papa?"

"No, that's my gramps."

"Can I see it again?" I looked closer and saw the edge of something white and shiny. "That a car?"

"Yeah, that's the one that came for me."

"What do you mean?"

"I mean, she came to look at my sis and me. It's a white car. The door opens, a woman comes out in a skirt, and she's got a lot of pens, notebooks, a bag full of papers." I look again and see horses in a pen in the background. There's a screen on their front door that shields the mess in the house behind them.

"They came to ask us questions, kept saying words like 'assessment' and 'foster.' My mom says Gramps was a good man, that he had to give us up because he was too old."

"You ever see him again?"

"Only in the newspaper," Tias remarked. "And only that I survived him."

X

I used to have long hair when I was a kid—my mom placed all her pride in it. To have a brown boy with hair that fell to the small of his back—that was her ceremony. She loved to comb and brush and braid it as I fell asleep on the couch watching Stuart on *MadTV* late night on weekends. My momma always took his words to heart: "Men are liars," which she'd repeat like a mantra. Stuart was the totem, the reminder, a promise that I would always be a boy who stuck by her side. I think she liked to picture us like that, me forever in pyjamas sliding down the bannister, and her warning me not to sack myself because that was all some men had going for them.

When I was young my kokum used to drive us into Selkirk where we would buy cheap clothes from the clearance racks of SAAN and shop for groceries at Extra Foods. I loved visiting that store because you had to pack your own bags and my kokum would let me push the button that worked the conveyor belt drawing cans of kidney beans and tins of baking soda toward us. My mom wasn't around whenever we went into Selkirk, she had errands to run around town, errands, I would later learn, that meant buying cheap booze from the Red Barn and collecting cocktails of painkillers. But shopping with my kokum in the Plaza, which really had only eight stores, was always my favourite kind of road trip. She'd let me visit the video store across from Extra Foods before we left and I'd browse through their bins of horror films and raunchy comedies. I was allowed to rent one movie every time and I always chose *Deuce Bigalow: Male Gigolo*. Gran and I would watch it on the weekends when she'd babysit me because my mom said Rob Schneider was a toad of a man who grossed her out, but my kokum thought he was hilarious. "Laughter is the sexiest thing," she'd say. I always wanted an aquarium like Deuce had, to have angel fish swimming around in it, and a loft with zebra print rugs and a chandelier in the entranceway. That was how you knew you had made it back in those days: animal prints and fancy candle holders. On the rez, we only ever had pelts, and our candles didn't have any holders, but were at least scented to mask the stink of shit and skins.

There was a Supercuts in the plaza where my kokum got her perms done. Usually I'd get a trim at the same time, to make room for new growth, like the Hutterites did when they set fire to their fields in the fall. This was an intimate time that my kokum and I shared, visiting the beauty parlour as she called it, even though a haircut usually only cost about ten dollars. This time, though, I told her I wanted my hair cut short like Brad Pitt, and she agreed to it, saying he was a good-looking man. So the hairdresser untied my braid and ran her fingers through my hair, untangling knots along the way, her hands as stiff as the prodding my mother did when she checked my hair for lice. She then gently pulled my hair together, tied it with an elastic, and with her shears started slicing through it like a utility knife fraying thick rope, shaking me out of my daze. Before I knew it my ponytail was on the floor, sad and static as a dragonfly whose wings had been plucked off. She then buzzed my sides and turned the top of my head into a shaggy faux-hawk. I liked watching her use her Spiker glue, making it tacky in her hands, then rubbing it through my hair to spike it up like a bed of nails. I felt as if I'd become a mace, a club, my head a deadly weapon rather than full of the soft strands my momma braided. I looked like the white boys who ran alongside their mothers playing Gameboys and Tamagotchis in the mall. My kokum said I looked very handsome. I asked the hairdresser if I could take my hair home. "Oh, for a cancer donation?" she asked. Without answering, I scooped it up and put it in my kokum's purse. She shook her head and said, "They all the same." The hairdresser gave us a weird stare while ringing us up at the till. My gran tipped her a few bucks so she'd fork over a lollipop to me.

My kokum had an obsession with whiteness. Momma says that when I was born, my kokum took me into her arms and inspected my hair, my eyes, my body, my little fingers wrapping around her ring finger like seaweed. "Oh, thank God," she said, "he looks white." Momma scooped me back up and lay me on her chest. "Thank the creator," she retorted, "he's Native." I can't fault my kokum for looking up to whiteness, hell, that woman had lived through some intense shit—most of which will remain unknown to me. That's her business and those were her strategies. I do look white sometimes, though, especially in winter when I'm not sun-kissed and my funds are too tight to afford any bronzer. My whiteness came in handy at times, less so at others; like when the rez boys loved to corner me at the band office to kick my ass for stealing their mommas' handouts. But whiteness got me here to Winnipeg, lets me enter gay bars without paying cover, lets me transform into different people on Snapchat because white is the base in every colour. When I used to hang out with the gays when I first moved to Winnipeg, the conversation of race was commonplace, and everyone would share examples of their grandparents' casual racism like, "Oh, she's pretty for a black girl," or talk about their obsessions with ancestry.com or 23andMe—tracking down the exact ingredients of their European genetic cocktails. Not that you really had to try that hard—I think white men have a different taste than Nates do; more pineapple and floral scents than Saskatoon jam and Lysol. DNA testing was like a rite of passage for them, they were obsessed with it, sent in vials of spit and swabs of cheeks to unknown places with cheques made out to god-knows-who, all so they could receive a piece of paper that proclaimed, "Here's who you are." How did they know it was correct? What made it any different than putting a dollar into a fortune-telling machine? Who says some algorithm wasn't randomly choosing countries and assigning them to you? And just how in the hell do white people have time to play around with their DNA, they must have a lot of free time, annit? They'd all discuss in great detail their great-great-great grandfathers with names like Seymour or MacDonald with such swollen pride as if they knew the fucker personally, as if that little piece of paper linked them back to christ or something. And of course some lousy kid would find out he was one twenty-fifth Cree and then call himself a proto-Hiawatha and lecture us all on Native issues. "We're all white here," my gays would say, then point towards me, the new NDN, "except you, but you look white, I mean, you're pretty much, you know?"

I never actually told them I was Native because I didn't want to have to out myself once again. If I did, they'd have started up a round of invasive questions, like a game of Guess Who, and I would sit there, never having been more violated than being the prize during a round of I Spy. You have to perform in any situation, so you may as well pick your battles. Hell, I played straight on the rez in order to be NDN and here I played white in order to be queer. You can't win in every situation, that's just the way it is. Best to avoid those topics, save your energy for when you're down to your last pack of cigarettes and ramen noodles. Shift when you need to—become your own best medicine. I think of my kokum when those conversations happen. "Thank God he's white." Thank someone, I'll think, whoever the hell is keeping me alive.

When my momma saw me with short hair and a faux-hawk, she cried harder than I'd ever heard her cry. "The fuck?" she said. "The fuck you do?" She called Kokum a goddamned curse and me a good-for-nothing. She bawled her eyes out, her face like the portrait of "The Scream," you would have thought someone had died. "You ruined him," she kept repeating through sobs, "you ruined my boy." Maybe a part of me did die that day, the day when the braid was severed from my head. But who knows? Maybe I'm like the NDN Athena, growing out of the head of Zeus, or hell, more like giving head to Zeus. My hair is the mediator between my selves, my spirits, my brownness and my queerness, my sexiness and my disgrace, the scar of all our pain.

XI

Fifty bucks would be enough cash to make my way to Selkirk—but I was looking for a ride back to Peguis and that was going to cost at least a couple hundred bills. If I had some cousins out here who actually liked me, I could probably bum a ride from them, but it's hard to convince these Rambo-bravado, gangster-wannabe thugs that they share any quantum of blood with an urban NDN, Two-Spirit femmeboy.

Roger, my mom's boyfriend, who she insisted I call stepdad, died from cirrhosis of the liver yesterday. He was a pigheaded, alcoholic, homophobic sonuva—but he made my mom happy, I don't know why or how, never cared to ask. Maybe it was because he sang Dolly Parton's "I Will Always Love You" to her at their wedding, which was less a wedding and more a tarp-covered jig-and-drink. Dolly was my mushom's favourite singer, and my mom used to tell me he'd sing it to her when she was a little girl. All the NDNs on the rez loved that song; it's like a rite of passage or something. Everyone in my family has taken a piece of Dolly. My mom took her lips, my real dad took her lyrics thinking he was always in the way and that was why he had to go, my kokum took her grace, and I took her body by becoming, what my clients like to call me, the best little whorehouse. It used to bother me, whore, but not so much anymore because, one: I don't sell sex, I sell fantasy and companionship; and two: when they call me what they call me it only helps me to know that I've found a home in my self. I learned that when I read this poem in high school by a dreary old white lady named Emily Dickinson. In it she calls herself nobody and asks the reader, "Who are you?" When our class first read that poem, they all laughed, thinking the line read, "I'm nobody, whore you?"

Then Kelly, one of the toughest NDN kids on the rez because he had six brothers and fifteen cousins, loudly announced, "Hey Hoover, sounds like *you*, you ol' cocksucker, you," and the whole class laughed. But so what if I liked sex, right? God, we all think about it; you're probably thinking about it right now. So I took these women and sewed them to myself like a tattered rag doll. I'm a little bit of Dolly and I'm a little bit of Em.

I'm nobody, whore you?

We're all here, like Em, on what she calls this undiscovered continent, hell, the reservation is a ghost-world, a prison, a death camp. Although, unlike Em, some of us just have deeper prisons on this undiscovered continent. There was me, feeling like the only gay NDN in the whole world, voguing and serving face in the basement of a reservation death camp situated in the farthest reaches of this undiscovered continent—now I tell my clients to dial "1" if they need me.

So anyway, Roger, my semi-stepdad, mostly-hated pseudo-father figure, yeah, he died yesterday and my mom called me to ask me to come to the funeral. I have two more days to get to the rez, which is about a five-hour drive away when combined with all the stops and pickups you'd have to take riding with a roundup driver. The wake will be going on until Friday, I'd never make it to that but, I told myself, I will make the funeral, I have to. Problem is, I have no money. I spent it all on some bronzer and banana powder at Sephora—I'm big into contouring these days, and a bit of bronzer really makes my cheekbones look like Maleficent, trust me, clients eat that shit up. So I have to earn nearly three hundred dollars in two days to raise enough funds to bum a ride and hitch my way back to the rez. Lord knows I didn't care about seeing Roger, truth be told—part of me is happy to see him go—but I have to be there for my mom. She's the *toughest* NDN in the world, I tell you, but I've seen how easily she broke when Roger went on his benders, so I can't even imagine how messed up she is feeling right now.

That, and I am dying, unconscious pun I swear, to visit my kokum again. On my birthday two years ago she called me and told me she needed to see me, that she had a story for me. See, my kokum is the first person in my family I've ever come out to, aside from my mom who I came out to a year later. And it was tough. I thought she would give me a lickin with her wooden spoon and tell me "Nononono!" But she just listened on the other end of the line while I cried into the receiver. All I could hear was her breathing deeply. When I eased up on the waterworks, it wasn't clear if she was still there—the line had gone silent. I wasn't sure if I was confessing to myself or maybe even some voyeur at MTS listening in on my conversation. Had she hung up? Was that the end of my kokum and me?

"Gran, you still there?"

"Mm-hmm," she replied, and as I hiccupped from all the crying, she asked, "You done, m'boy, or what?"

When I caught my breath and softly answered yes, she laughed. "Heck, like I didn't even know, Jonny. Why you think I gave you them earrings last year?"

"Because I told you I needed them for art class?"

"Jonny, m'boy, your kokum old but she ain't dull. You's napêwisk-wewisehot, m'boy, Two-Spirit. You still my beautiful baby grandkid no matter what you want to look like or who you want to like."

I wanted to question her on what she meant by Two-Spirit, but she cut me short by yelling that she had to go, her frybread oil was ready.

"You come down here, m'boy, and I'll tell you a story about who you are. You come and you'll know. Kihtwâm, m'boy, kisâkihitin."

It's funny, NDN families only seem to reconvene when someone's dead. It doesn't take much to make an NDN cry, but a death, that makes them stoic as all hell; well, stoic and maybe hungry. You'll never have a better meal than at an NDN funeral.

And that's the truth.

XII

My kokum used to babysit me a lot when I was a kid whenever my mom was down at the Royal, celebrating everything from birthdays to just surviving the week. I didn't mind; I loved sleeping over. She tried to teach me how to bead, but my fingers didn't have the dexterity to push a needle through something so tiny. We'd bake pies and she'd tell me to take two home, one for me, one for my momma for when she woke up. I loved exploring her basement, my kokum was a hardcore hoarder and kept everything everyone ever gave her. All of our Christmas presents, birthday gifts, all the knick-knacks we gave her were stored down there. And if I didn't crash on her couch and watch reruns all night, I usually slept in the basement on a mattress, a makeshift bedroom barricaded in by years' worth of gifts. My kokum had a hilarious way of gift-giving—she'd often re-gift you what you gave her a year or two earlier if she hated it or was mad at you, but on the other hand if you were in her good books, she'd give you something she made herself. She was always knitting pot holders and wash cloths, much to my mom's annoyance— we had drawers full of them.

One Christmas my mom took us to Selkirk to shop for gifts. I was on the hunt for the perfect present for Kokum and made my way into this Hallmark store which was full of journals, cards, and ornaments. I browsed up and down every aisle with the fifteen dollars I had saved up from three months' worth of allowance and rolled coins. There were all sorts of random things in there: crystals, rocks, little dream catchers for your car, and a whole row of glass animals. There was one in particular that I liked, this frog in a straw hat lying against a rock, fishing in a little pond. I was eyeing it up when the cashier came over to me.

"Do you want to take a closer look at it?" She bent down and unlocked the glass case it was in, then held it out for me to look at. I looked that glass frog in the eye, and after much deliberation, I decided that this was the one.

"How much?" I asked.

She looked at the tag. "$34.99," she said. I followed her to the register and pulled out the two fives I had, then spilled the rolls of coins I had saved up all over the counter.

"Is this enough?"

Just then my mom came into the store. "Here you are, heck, I've been looking for you for like twenty minutes."

The cashier laughed. "I'll let you two talk it over," she said, and busied herself with another customer.

"Mom, can I buy this?"

"This thing? What for?"

"For Kokum."

"The hell is she gonna do with this?" She took a closer look, then saw the price. "Thirty-five dollars for a frog? You know how many things we could buy for that?"

"I think she'll like it," I said, and tugged on her hand. I had this weird way of lacing myself into my mom whenever she was mad at me. I'd stand on her toes, put my head beneath her shirt, stare up at her breasts, and twine my fingers into hers. When I did it in public, she'd usually get mad.

"Not today, Jonny, put it back—we can't afford it."

And I burst into tears, and boy, did I cry. I scooped up my money off the counter, stormed out of the store, and ran to the nearest bathroom, where I locked myself in a stall to sulk. When I came out my mom was waiting for me, keys in hand, with a bag from SAAN.

On our way back to the rez, we stopped in Teulon for a couple cans of pop. Before continuing on, my mom handed me a piece of gum and turned the radio off.

"You know, Jonny, we can't always get what we want," she said.

"I know, Momma, it's just—I saved up all this money to shop."

"I saw, look at all that cash, good on you."

"Whatchu think I can get Kokum, then? Can you help me make her something?"

She nodded toward the SAAN bag on the backseat. "Just reach in, for godsakes, don't go snooping around." I put my hand inside and pulled out the frog wrapped in bubble wrap. "Don't tell Rog, okay?" she said.

I cradled the frog for a minute before placing it back inside the bag, then lunged at my mom and hugged her. "I love you, Momma, I just love you!" I said, making her swerve the car across the road.

"Cut the shit, Jonny, you're gonna make me crash." I scooched back over to my seat and pulled out my cash.

"Here's my money," I said, "to help pay."

"Nah, m'boy. You earned it, you keep it."

She pulled me toward her and eventually I fell asleep with her arm around me. When we got home I wrapped that frog in a gym bag

I had sewed in home ec and hid it for three weeks, trying my hardest not to go and blab to Kokum that I got her something right nice. And that old frog's still up in her living room, covered in dust; he's been sitting there fishing for years now, sitting beside a picture of my kokum and Mush.

Kokum and I did all sorts of crazy shit when she babysat me. She used to tell me scary stories about the wendigo and Nanabush, stories about ghosts and aliens. She had an obsession with horror and was dead set that she would see Bigfoot at least once in her life. Once she took me out into the bush late at night, like she used to do with my uncles, flashlights in hand, to look for him.

"People say they saw him, y'know, right here in these woods," she said. As we explored the nooks and crannies of the bush, she told me all about how she once saw a UFO, saw it with all of its lights coming straight toward her home before it suddenly took off up and over to the north. "You know," she said, stopping me and grabbing my hand so our flashlights were pointing up at the sky, "they say there was a UFO crashing that night in Jackhead. Military and all, buncha people got asked to evacuate, weird eh?" We continued on through the bush, forging our own damn paths because my kokum was a bad ass like that. We never did find Bigfoot, but we did find a lot of trap lines and even a lynx that was snared, slowly dying in the night.

Sometimes we listened to her favourite song, "Come and Get Your Love" by Redbone. Heck, when we did, we used to throw on her old shawls and dance around as the adults sang. "Hell, what the matter with your head?" they'd sing and Kokum said my dancing looked like the fancy shawl dance, but I thought I looked more like an epileptic groundhog. The shawls were too big for me and the fabric draped beneath my feet, but we danced however the hell the song directed us to—jumping in the middle of the living room, hopping off the couches, spinning in circles with our arms splayed like airplanes, and the fabric twirling so fast that all we saw were brief flashes of our faces through the blur.

And then I guess one time I got too close to the steps and fell down the stairs, face forward down fourteen steps, cracked my collarbone. But I was still full of endorphins, didn't feel the pain right away, just sat there looking up at my kokum whose face was full of horror, her hands cupped around her cheeks, her mouth saying "M'boy" over and over beneath the roar of the music, "Come and get your love, come and get your love, come and get your love now" repeating.

When my mom came to pick me up two days later, she freaked out. "The fuck? He did what?" She yelled at my kokum for what seemed like hours.

"You're good for nothing, you know that? Nothing!" she screamed at her.

"I didn't mean—he fell."

"How the hell you let a boy crack his damn neck?"

I tried to intervene. "Mommy, I didn't crack—"

"Hush up," she said, then turned back to my kokum. "Boy, I can't even trust you to watch my boy for one goddamn night."

And then my kokum was crying with a loud wail that wracked my bones with aches, a vibrato that buzzed on my clavicle, stung me good. I clung to her apron, holding tightly onto her with my good arm, as my mom pulled me off her and forced me up the stairs. She didn't realize she was pulling on me where my arm was slung. I yelled for Kokum and heard her crying at the bottom of the stairs. As we were about to leave, she ran up.

"You take care of that boy, Karen, you damn well hear me?" She pushed her words out with laboured breath.

"Hmph, you want me to take advice from the woman who broke my baby?"

"Least I was here, Karen. At least I was here."

My mom glared at her and balled up her fists, but then she just opened the door and we left. For the next two weeks she babied me, made me Cup-a-Soup, rented us scary movies—and saved up all her energy to find a way to apologize to Kokum. I had to wear the sling for a couple weeks; the fall left me with a dent in my clavicle, wide enough to contain both of those women's many tears.

XIII

I threw my iPod on and made my way down Portage to snatch up a cheap bottle of OJ from the Dollar Tree. Florence Welch was belting "The dog days are over" into my ears. Hard to believe, I thought, on the very street where Idle No More thrummed and flashdanced and marched—in the very mall where they were arrested. *Môniyâw*, I thought, so disillusioning. I strutted by the Marlborough where that Nate boy, Pratt, went missing, the same night that I too was walking by there. All the Nates down the street were wearing plaid jackets ripped at their seams, their white shirts stained with Lucky and spit and piss and the grime of Winnipeg. That sweet yellow smoke that foxed their skin like an old tome—gotta make your way into those museums if you want to survive. I wondered what would happen if I sat down here on the stoops of the hotels, passing around hooch and comparing boils and skin tags and all things that look diseased but pass as a normal NDN aesthetic. Would you walk by me like a dog unleashed but too lost to sniff his way back home? Implement drones to monitor the streets and arrest suspicious-looking types?

"I want my twenty dollars," a man in a muumuu yelled, his hair a crown of thistles, thin, stringy, tangled, his beard serving major lumbersexual realness. "I need to buy her groceries." He's always yelling this; old Abraham we call him, because he's the rare Native who can grow facial hair—an emancipatory act if there ever was one.

There was this big ol' NDN girl on the rez named Abraham too—and she had this one cousin, Conner, a real wannabe thug who always thought he was being tracked by the FBI. He was almost as bad as my own aunty who truly believed she was visited and probed by aliens on a regular basis—paranoia is a type of exchange on the rez. Conner and Abraham's cousin was named Colton, a real annoying punk who used to like to corner me with Abraham at the bingo hall where we hung out and drank. He only really started to hate me after I gave him a hand job at his birthday sleepover after a few weeks of online sexting. And holy hell, let me tell you, when that boy came he damn near drug up the whole of the Assiniboine with him.

When everyone would go home for the night, Tias and I used to hang back and make out in the bushes. Everyone knew but no one acknowledged it, they were all happy enough to leave two faggot boys to tinker with each other so long as we were out of sight, out of mind. Connor, Abraham, and Colton, the three cousins, once caught us, though, and started pelting us with rocks. Tias and I managed to escape and we booked it through the backroads to my kokum's, out of breath, sweating, our backs sore and bleeding. These adrenaline rushes were a daily high for me. I liked to think that I was Jean Grey and Tias was my Cyclops, the two of us fighting off the Shi'ar Imperial Guard in a match to determine who would die and who would live. I imagined me in that tight little green costume with the bright yellow visor and him in a skin-tight blue suit showing off that glorious bulge between his legs. We'd both be backed into a corner as waves of enemies showered us with concussion grenades and psionic light beams. Old Jean Grey protecting her man with a force field she struggled to keep up against the constant fight. I wondered if we were like that, two mutant boys shielding one another from all the things that wanted to martyr us—how long could we hold out? Of course, old Jean Grey ended up dead at the end of the episode, but me, well, I was still a young buck with a whole lot of hate and an endless supply of energy. It's easy to run yourself into the ground, but maybe that ain't such a bad thing? Jean Grey became the M'Kraan Crystal, didn't she? What type of jewel would I become?

"You got twenty dollars?" the muumuu man asked me, his eyes staring down at the sidewalk.

"Sorry, bud. Here's a cig."

"Thanks, kid," he said, his eyes now locked onto mine, looking too much like two black holes, all stippled with sunspots like he went up and swallowed a sundog whole. Part of me wanted to crawl up inside those eyes, yell out "Daddy!" and hear only the echo of my voice. But I didn't, what else was Winnipeg but a giant galactic shithole sucking everything into its white mass, its dwarf stars.

"Don't sweat it," I said.

I told myself that I would double, if not triple, the number of clients over the next two days so I could make enough money to get home. I also needed enough to cover my rent, to pay back Ernie for the ounce of weed, and then the travel money on top of that. My body was going to hurt, but I remember reading a Shakespeare play at school once that said it takes a pound of flesh to earn a pound of cash. As my momma used to say, if anyone could do it, it would be me, cuz I'm stubborn as a mule and strong as a bear. I guess I was running, like Florence said, fast for my mother, and away from my father; the squaw days aren't over.

XIV

On the rez my aunty lived a good kilometre or two away from my kokum's house. I loved visiting her; her house was small but cozy— the scents of old wood and the dry warmth of her oven, the sound of a screen door screeching closed, and crackling branches, the howl of winter winds. She wasn't much of a talker, but she was one hell of a listener—I would go there and tell her stories for hours at a time. She'd always nod and smile, but when I told her something funny she'd laugh out loud, her whole body jiggling.

Aunty's best dish was her hangover soup. Hell, all the family would come there on Sunday, fresh off a treaty day's bender, and gorge on her soup. It was made from beef stock and canned tomato soup and had huge chunks of hamburger, or stewing beef if it was welfare week, and plump macaroni noodles. Of course there was also celery, carrots, onions, and sometimes potatoes—but because every NDN I knew was as carnivorous as could be, sometimes we scooped up only the meat and broth into our bowls. We'd also tear off giant slabs of her famous bannock and smother it in butter and jam—god, that shit was delicious. One time she asked me to knead her bannock because her fibromyalgia was hurting her, but she quickly took over because I didn't have the stamina to knead more than a few minutes—now, every time I knead bannock, I'm reminded of how strong the women in my family are. As we ate, my uncle would crack open another beer and say, "Hair of the dog, y'know?" while others would be smoking up a storm and butting out their cigarettes in an empty Diet Pepsi can.

The men and women would split up into different circles to exchange stories from the weekend, usually about who they snagged, but told it with different manners. The men talked about how suave they were, with amazing pickup lines like "Hey girl, I ain't no one-minute-man, I'm on NDN time, eh." Slack old jokes. The women, on the other hand, would tell on who they ended up fighting with, or which man they had to slap away. But there were tender stories too, like how they took care of someone if they got too drunk.

It was always terrifying trying to get to my aunt's place, though; I'd have to walk down this empty backroad and I was always afraid of being attacked by a bear. One time, when I slept over, we woke up in the morning to the sound of crumpling tin and a loud thud on her wooden porch. We peeked out the window to investigate and found a black bear sitting next to her garbage can, eating a banana peel. And my aunt, tiny as she was, and in her paper-thin nightgown, picked up her corn broom and stormed outside in the cold January air. She was fearless, that woman; she walked outside barefoot and marched right up to that bear and struck him on the nose with her broom, once, twice, bam. And then that great bear stood up on its hind legs, its claws the length of scissors, and grunted; but my aunt, tough as nails, smacked that bear again on its head and yelled at the top of her voice, "Git! G'wan you, out, out, git!" The bear stared at her quizzically for a few seconds, then lowered himself and jogged back into the bush. My aunt came back inside, her feet red as the beans she cooked in her chili, and dusted herself off as if it was nothing, then went about her morning routine of frying up bologna and yesterday's mashed potatoes. That was the only time in my life I heard her yell—and lord, I would never want to be on the other end of that vicious scream of hers. If it can scare away a bear, I knew it had the volume to chase away men and redcoats too.

My aunty always told me that if I ever ran into a bear, to stand my ground to avoid being attacked. Whenever I heard a twig snap, I'd jump around and get into my most aggressive bear stance—but most times it was a squirrel or else my kokum's cat, Jynx. That old cat loved to play tricks and since I always fed her my leftovers she followed me everywhere. Her favourite game seemed to be "Scare-the-fuck-out-of-Jonny-as-he-walks-home." She would creep up behind me and pounce on my legs when I was least expecting it. And when I got home, she would make loud noises that sounded more like giggles than meows.

My aunty's advice came in handy when I finally did run into a bear. It was pretty small, but when I tell the story it's as giant as the one in *The Revenant*. Anyway, it looked fierce as fuck when it stormed out of the bush while I was walking and sat down on the road ahead of me. I instantly thought of that ol' bear statue at the zoo, Winnie—but I wasn't no cavalry vet, I was more like a Christopher Robin. As it sat there staring at me, my aunty's warnings ran through my head: "Stare 'em in the eyes, stomp your feet, hell, take a step forward if you have to, be big." So I stared back at him. His eyes were as dark as my mom's skin, and he had a little patch of white fur on his chest that looked like one hell of a deformed butterfly. I stomped my feet but he didn't stir, he only stuck his tongue out the side of his mouth, his perky little ears standing at attention. I raised my hands above my head to make myself look bigger, but that didn't work, it only made him get off his ass and take a few steps toward me, his large floppy tongue bouncing with each step he took. As he moved closer, I began to panic, and thought of the other warning my aunty taught me: "Make noise." "Git!" I screamed, but my voice cracked like a pubescent teen, and the bear stood his ground. So I got my iPod out and hit play; the first song that came on was Nirvana's "Heart-Shaped Box." I turned up the volume to maximum and started running toward the bear. He backed off and ran to the side of the road, afraid of the cavalcade of voices coming through my earphones; I guess he thought I was walking with ghosts? He was still staring at me as I ran past him, as fast as my legs could carry me to my aunty's house. I turned around and saw that the bear was now lying in the road on its back, and for some reason its penis was erect as all hell. When I told my aunty what had happened, she looked outside her window and saw the bear lying in the road and had a good ol' laugh. "For godsakes, m'boy, that's just a cub." I didn't say anything else, just went into her spare room and listened to that Nirvana song on repeat until I fell asleep. I wondered if it was the right thing to do to scare the bear like that—can you scare a bear into an erection? Did I have a right to summon ghosts? Hell, I was like that NDN shaman, Taylor, in *Poltergeist*; heck, I often talk to myself and wonder if I'm really talking with myself or if I'm conversing with spirits. I guess I'm always "forever in debt to your priceless advice."

XV

The best advice I've ever received was from my mom when I was eight. See, my momma is the toughest NDN in the world—a real hard-ass, but the kind you need, the kind who can break rocks and divine rivers. She walked into my room all casual-like, her hair knotted into a ratty bun and wearing the gold glitter of Elvis's face on her T-shirt caulked with flour. She took a liking to a thunderbird I was beading.

"Who's that for?" she asked.

"No one," I shrugged. Little did she know that I was actually making it to give as a gift to Brayden Walker—the first boy I ever liked. Brayden was a common Nate name, but that's what you get when you live on the rez: a million Braydens, sixteen Jasmines, and a little femme-boy-fatale named Jonny. Momma picked up the bird I was making and held it up against the window to inspect it. The little beads dangled in the dusty afternoon light, and its form created a shadowy inverse thunderbird on the floor—a great half-winged creature on the carpet not two feet from the stain from a Budweiser can.

"You know your dad was a whatchamacallit?"

"Thunderbird?"

"Yeah, that's the one. It's good," she finally said. "Real good. What you making off it?"

"Nothing," I replied. "It's a gift."

"Boy, you better be kidding me."

When I shook my head, she furrowed her brow, revealing the chickenpox scars above her temples. That was how you knew she was *real* mad—a deep oval imprint that hid beneath the lines in her skin, looking like an angry eye. "Work like this? Boy—you're something, you know that? Really something. Don't you ever let me catch you doing this again."

I asked her what she meant, half shaking, thinking she knew about Brayden and that she'd reach for her wooden spoon and give me a lickin like the schoolyard boys used to do when they'd swipe at me with their hand-me-down shoes and dirty fingernails. "You're Ogla-la," they'd tell me, "not some fairy city boy." When they walked away, I used to mutter beneath my breath, "No, it's ooh-*la-la*," and vogue in the blood and sand. Really, I was neither—I was Oji-Cree—but to them it was all the same.

"You're good with your hands," she said. "And people notice that. If you want to survive out there, boy, you got to learn how to sell yourself. Work like this? Shit, you could earn an easy ten dollars selling it to them touristy white folk. Hell, maybe twenty if you looked sad enough. Listen, m'boy, if you're good at something, don't you ever go doing it for free, you hear me? When you grow up, you're gon' learn all sorts of things—find what you good at and put a number to it, you hear? And when you get that number, you double it. That how you gonna make it. Lord ain't give you these skills so that you be making them for no punk that don't give two hoots about you. Don't be thinking I don't know who this for—you like that Walker boy. I'm fine with that, son, Creator, he made you for a reason—you girl and you boy and that's fine with me, but what's not fine is you selling yourself short. You gotta leave if you wanna survive, and when you do you're gonna need the steadiness of those hands, m'boy. You're gonna need a rock and a whole lotta medicine."

Momma's lesson is one I'd hold dear from that moment on—me, the rock breaker? Ain't no NDN glitter princess ever been called that, heck, I was more like the one who got them off.

XVI

I drew myself a bath, my tub the grungy yellow of cigarette-stained fingers, hairs clinging to its sides and perimeter. As I sat down in it, I thought of the Red River that gushed blood and guts and catfish a few blocks away. I wondered how cold the rapids in Peguis were right now, those fat leeches waiting for a fish to suckle off; here, my penis, wriggling in the bath, I too am cheap tackle. Those frothy waters full of Lucky cans and severed hands and oak leaves that clogged our drain pipes.

Water was a mentor to me, a playmate; water was a feral child. I used to sit on the bank of the rapids, feet dangling in the stream. If I stayed still long enough, the crawfish would climb over them, inspect the grooves between my toes. What would life be like if I were a crawfish? A little pest that ages too fast, only three months and then they're plunged into the cruel world of adulthood. To be a crawfish is to be in constant fear of your own self, to be ripped apart by kin who pierce your soft spots with teeth and claws that shred you from the inside out. To be a crawfish, I thought, is the best primer for survival; if you can make it as a crawfish, you can make it as anything. I plucked the crawfish from my toes, let the water have it, let it fumble, scramble, try to live; the rapids are an apocalyptic *Mad Max* landscape. I watched it catch its groove, then tumble into the ducts and disappear. Who knows where it would end up? I hoped it would continue living, even if only one more day, but who really knows these things. The water is a furious road and the only words we can say to one another are simple: witness me.

The water in Winnipeg was just as feral as the rapids in Peguis—the only difference was that this river ate children, not crawfish. My kokum told me that Manitoba was a name taken from the Cree, manitowapow, which meant something like "the strait of the spirit." She said it was the sound of the drum, of water beating the rocks in a constant thrum, noise like a round dance where the water would ask you to sing alongside it. The river is a space of convergence, where streams and currents intersect briefly, an orgy of kissing streams, a hub of sex and slapping fins. The water is the colour of rust, the kind of rust that becomes a sequin when a raindrop hovers over it. When I look out over the Red I see the strait, but I wonder just what in the hell a spirit is doing out there. How many Manito? Was mine out there too? Why would the water want to straighten my spirit? Ain't that why I have two?

The elders used to tell us to humble ourselves to the water; I heard them in the speeches of Immortan Joe: "Do not become addicted to water." But water was always a shameful thing for me: to piss, to sweat, to spit, to ejaculate, to bleed, to cry. How in the hell do we humble ourselves to water when we're so damn humiliated by it? Life ain't always as easy as an old story that never changes, y'know? And we weren't always so embarrassed of ourselves as water; we were basins of thought too once. Bathing was a tumultuous experience when I was a kid. My mom would run me a bath, but the water would be the temperature of the lava in *Dante's Peak*. I would feel like Granny Ruth paddling through acidic volcanic liquid in my mother's bath water, my legs turning pink and tingling, the heat stinging my nose, all the while my mother reassuring me it's "not even hot." Then she would climb in, her tummy and breasts falling loose in the water, her stretch marks like footprints on her belly and hips. She'd nestle me in between her legs and ease us both back into it, the hot water cradling us, covering my chest, opening up my lungs, my exhales a steady stream of dirt and mucus and phlegm that purged themselves from my body. And her hair, her long brown hair, snaked around the tub, wrapping itself around my arms, making me look like I too had hair the length of a horse's tail. My mother would wash us both with L'Oréal kids shampoo, the watermelon kind, a green bottle with a pink lid, and an eye peeking out at us from the label. It was the shampoo that never burned my eyes, Momma assured me of that. And while we lathered up our hair, I built myself a pair of breasts just like my mother's using the soap from my head. "Momma, you think I'm pretty?" I'd ask and she'd reply, "M'boy, ain't no one ever looked better."

We'd cuddle in the tub until the water turned cold and opaque, until our nipples turned to points and our fingers pruned like Kokum's. My mom would get out first and I'd remain in the water, gurgling it in my mouth, the taste of soap, dirt, skin, sweat—I drank it in small sips until my belly felt hard as a rock. I liked to put my head beneath the water, listen to time slowing down, the sound of my blood pulsing in my head, the distorted voices of Roger and Mom arguing downstairs, the enhanced sound of their footsteps which made their own music, gave their own cues. In the water I was beautiful: my boy body was genderless in the tub, my penis too shrivelled to really look like anything but the nether regions of a Barbie doll, my nipples shielded by a facecloth, covering a shame that would never be mine. The water never set me straight.

The water leaked with me down the drain.

Here, in my own bathtub alone, I think of Momma, I think of those rapids. I think of how they split rocks and dissolved them into sand; I think of how water crafted this whole damn planet, carved it into animals. I think of home. Just why in the hell did I ever decide to leave? Kokum's gone and Momma's got the sickness of loneliness, the kind that'll turn your liver into coal. Leaving made me feel as if I'd split myself; this throb, a residue of pride, having left—for the life of me, all I wanted now was this: to regress, to crawl backwards into time, into a womb that smells of earthworms and eggshells, for my knowledge of the world and its pains to be a second thought; for my idea of home being bound by only four walls on the rez. All I wanted was to shift back up inside my mother in the bath water of her uterus, to count time as a crawfish would, for days to mean something other than another notch on the wall, another treaty dollar earned. I wanted that. I wanted all of that. How easy, how warm, how outlandishly impossible, I thought. Just how in the hell are we supposed to live in a world that ages us like fish? I washed my hair with Head and Shoulders, killed the bugs that were making a life on my scalp. I felt my self in the tub, my blood stiffened to a point, made my own throbbing drumbeat, my own manitowapow, my own round dance being the huff of breath you make when the nerves on your cock tingle like Pop Rocks. I came into my bathwater, let the residue swim and eventually drown in the tub.

"If you come back," I said, "don't ever come back as an NDN, y'hear?"

XVII

I sometimes have this dream where I'm walking around naked in the mountains—it's spring and the purple seeds in the pods begin to open up and bloom into a lilac. Bees buzz around it, their wings slicing through the air, their bodies velvet smooth in a way that reminds me of how I like to shave my pubes. The buds drip a lavender dew and even the rods are golden and erect. All the land is horny as fuck. The treaty land has awakened and the berries are thick with juice that threatens to burst out of their infant seeds. Butterflies swarm in a patch of sunlight, their wings a collective noise that sounds like crinkling plastic or a consistent, hearty fap. Little squirrels gather nuts around me and a doe walks by with her fawns, the little ones suckling on their mother's leather nipples. Their fur is a rich brown and their spots remind me of the war paint I've seen in movie westerns.

The earth is moist from an early morning rain, the grass glittering like glass. In the mud there is a set of prints: something with long sharp claws. Maskwa, I think, he has come. I tear one of my cigarettes in half, pour the tobacco over the prints, lay my hand on top of it, and press it into the earth. I wonder if Manito is hearing me say over and over and over: kisâkihitin. And this round dance song comes into my head—I don't know when I've ever heard it, but I know the words in this dream, I don't have to Google it. The constant thump of the drum sounds like a rabbit's leg pounding on stretched deer skin. I am on all fours to fit my hands into the prints as I push the tobacco down far-ther—down as deep as I can, into the breast of askîy. As I push, twigs and little stones cut my hands, and blood pools into the mud, seeps into my lacerations. I taste soil in my mouth.

A branch snaps behind me. I don't turn around but stay low to the ground, hovering on all fours, penis dragging in the mud. A warm breath snakes down the nape of my neck and a fat black tongue works its way through the grooves of my cartilage. It probes my ear and the suction from its tongue pulls on my lobe. The tension reminds me of my kokum when she plays with my ears. A fuzzy chest presses against my bare back—the weight forces me down into the mud, and part of me wonders if this is nôhtâwiy. The song of the round dance grows louder in my ears, unfiltered by the tongue that scrapes and cleans me—wabanonong manidoo owaabamaan anishinaabek. I can't help but cry—I don't understand the words but my tendons do, my bones react and jig in the skin. The beat doubles, rabbit and beaver thwack in conversation. I feel something hard press against the small of my back—zhaawanong manidoo owaabamaan anishinaabek. He places his paws on top of my hands, they feel like the bottom of my mom's mocs. Then his claws press into the tips of my fingers, piercing them, blood and foam leaking out from my fingertips—ningaabii'anong manidoo owaabamaan anishinaabek. All of the forest is watching maskwa top me as the birds cackle and avert their eyes. A woodpecker sits high in a tree and riddles the trunk with a beat that dubs the round dance—kiiwedinong manidoo owaabamaan anishinaabek. Maskwa unsheathes himself, the baculum stiff and ready; he enters me with a hefty breath and it doesn't hurt. I wonder if he's getting ready to eat me. He digs through my body, feels for the bean in me,

70

buzzes against it, looks for the bone that holds my tapwewin. I tell him there's nothing there, but he scrapes from me a seed from when I was kikâwiy, anishinaabek-nehiyaw iskwewayi-napêw. And as he pulls out, he jiggles the bean again, makes me come into the mud, licks the salt from my eyes—all of this treaty land is filled with me. As he leaves, the music fades, my heart-drum-beat lulls to a slow pace, my body relaxes, lets loose its fluids. Kâkike, he huffs, kisâkihitin kâkike.

When I've hurt my Cree, well—still, I dream of maskwa.

XVIII

Gym class was something I always loathed as a kid. I was one of the "shy guys" who'd change in the bathrooms, or hang back until everyone else was finished showering, or else earn myself another Emmy by faking a cold. I was chubby as all hell and the other boys used to whip me with towels or climb over the stalls and make fun of me changing. Once, I worked up the courage to change alongside them, and they shied away. "What are you looking at, perv?" one of them asked, and then they all changed beneath their towels or behind locker doors. All my uncles had round bellies with marks that looked like scrapes; I thought they looked beautiful, sexy even. Tias would sometimes hang back with me; sometimes we'd skip out together and smoke with the Bad Girls, other times he'd wait to change alongside me.

After baseball practice once, we stayed back as usual, pretending to look for something I'd lost. Our teacher just rolled his eyes and went inside as all the other boys filed in like restless bear cubs, jumping on one another. Whenever a couple of them started a fight, the other boys would throw off their shirts, form a circle, and chant, "Fight!" The two boys would circle one another, hunched low to the ground, fists moving like shifting eyes. "Skoden," they'd say back and forth, jutting out their chins and lips. And coach would never stop them. "Boys," he'd say, "what you gonna do?"

After we figured the boys were finished their showers, Tias and I went inside. We watched each other undress, but our bodies were nothing new, no need to compare them because those geographies had already been explored. But I loved how delicately he undressed, neatly folding his shorts and shirt, then wrapping a towel around his waist, his hair tousled like a feral. We showered and as we did I followed the way the water drained over his body, snaking down his chest, threading around his penis, and pooling beneath his soles which were thick as deer hide from running around barefoot all the time. And when he held his hands out, the water would drain down his arms and pour from his fingertips.

Sometimes I'd go to his house when his parents went out to bingo and hired a babysitter. I never understood why they had a babysitter, every other NDN family I knew had a ton of cousins who'd watch your kids for a few bucks. The babysitter's name was Ginny. She was a few years older than us and always planned games for us to play. She'd also bring over movies like *Dumb and Dumber* and *Spice World*. We watched those films a million times, quoted them like lifelines. When Tias would get mad at me, I'd just repeat à la Lloyd Christmas, "Tias...I took *care* of it," and that was all we needed to resolve the argument. Ginny liked to give us makeovers and colour our nails so we could be posh too—a tradition we wholeheartedly signed up for. We'd play with lipsticks and eyeliners, then paint her over too, like a half-assed version of Elisha Cuthbert. And she made sure to clean our faces off before Tias's parents got home.

But it was nail painting we loved the most. How she'd prep our nails with alcohol, ask us which colour we wanted. Our favourite was this silver-glitter one that shone in the light when it was dry.

"That's right boss," Tias would proudly exclaim when she was done, examining his fingers.

Ginny would slide the brush over our nails with this stern exactitude, her eyes squinting. She never second-guessed herself, and I always wondered how she could be so precise. Every time I tried to do anything so determined, my body would tremble and my head would throb; I never had a damn chance at winning a round of Operation because of it. One, two, three slides of the brush and our fingers were transformed into high glamour, like the Sailor Scouts we used to watch on TV. And then she'd apply a layer of gloss that really made them shine. "Whew," she'd say, fanning the air with her hands, "this stuff is strong." Tias and I used to breathe in the scent of the paint, which cleared our nostrils and let us pretend we were high.

As meticulous as we were about cleaning everything up before Tias's parents got home, one night they came home early, his dad a little drunk and a little salty at losing at bingo again. As they pulled up in the driveway, Ginny quickly cleaned up all her makeup, turned off the movie, and told us to go wash up. We tried to scrub off the paint as quick as we could, but we had let it dry too much while we were all dancing to the Spice Girls. Ginny tried to stall them at the door.

"How was yer night?" she asked.

"Same old same, dear," Tias's mom said, draping her coat over a chair.

"Fucking waste of time and money, if you ask me," his dad announced. "Who the hell stands a chance of winning when you got a whole row of old-ass women dabbing like goddamn machines?"

Ginny laughed. "Yeah, they're pretty good, eh?"

"Good? Goddamn cheaters," he said, throwing his keys onto the table. "At least the drinks are cheap at the hall, though."

"Oh, hey Gin, do you mind if we pay you next week?" his mom asked. "We had to gas up with our last twenty."

"Oh yeah, that's cool." Ginny put on her coat and grabbed her backpack. Tias's mom offered to give her a lift home, which she accepted.

Once they were gone, his dad sat down on the couch and turned the TV channel to ESPN as we inched our way slowly into the living room, our hands in our pockets. "What you boys do tonight?" he asked and we shot-the-shit, told him we watched TV and played some video games. Tias went over to hug him.

"Don't ever play bingo, boys, y'hear? Save your money."

"All right," Tias replied, pushing himself out of the hug.

His dad looked down at Tias's hands. "The hell's that?"

"What?" Tias said, putting his hands back into his pockets.

His dad pulled them out. "You boys painting your nails?"

"Oh, that's just paint from school, must have gotten on me."

I tried to interject. "Yeah, we did this—"

He pulled Tias's hands up to his nose. "Don't know what you two think you're doing lying to me." He let go of Tias's hands, then stared at the TV for a minute. We thought we were good. We scurried back to his room and sighed with relief.

"Close one, eh?" I said.

"Tias, get your ass out here right now!" his dad yelled from the kitchen. Tias gulped, got up, and told me to stay in the room. But I followed, peeking out from behind the wall. I saw his dad with a pair of nail clippers in his hand.

"How many fucking times I tell you to cut this girly shit, huh?"

"I'm sorry, we—"

Before Tias could finish, his dad snatched his hand from his pocket and pushed it down on the counter, held his fingers out with his, and began cutting.

"You gotta stop hanging around that girly-boy, y'hear me?"

I could hear the sharp clip of metal on nail. When he cut one too short, Tias winced. "Oh, shut up, this is nothing," his dad said, and kept on cutting until Tias's fingers were bleeding.

"Oh, grow some goddamn balls," his dad said. I started to come out from hiding but caught Tias's eyes, and he shook his head no. We held each other's gaze; his teeth were clenched and he made quick inhalations through the little gaps between them, his eyes squinting every time the clipper cut off another layer of nail and skin. "Run?" I mouthed to him. But his dad saw me and pointed the clippers at me. "You want some of this too, boy? Mind your business." When he was finally finished, Tias just stood there, his eyes two vacant holes.

"There," his dad said. "That looks a hell of a lot more manly." He threw a dishcloth at Tias and told him to wrap his fingers up, keep pressure on them. "Quit fucking 'round, y'hear?" he said, and went back to the couch, sat himself in that all-too-familiar ass-groove. Tias wiped up the spots of blood and bits of nail from the counter and then we both returned to his room. We unwound the cloth and looked at his hands. One nail was split wide open, cut straight down to the bed: a bloody, mushy layer that looked like an exposed brain. We sat side by side, and I rested my head on his shoulder.

"It's kinda cool, eh?" Tias said.

"Yeah," I replied, "makes you look a zombie!"

He huffed. "He's not my real dad, y'know?"

"I know," I said, patting his back.

He cleaned his fingers very delicately in the shower, making gentle circles over the skin with soap. When he was finished, he saw me watching him, the sound of the hockey announcer on TV a muted lull beneath the roar of his father's shouting. "What?" Tias said. I went over to him, took his hand, and stuck his finger in my mouth. The skin had hardened and felt tough on the tongue, but there were still soft spots at the nailbed.

"The fuck?" he said and tried to shove me off, but then stopped himself, breathed in, closed his eyes, and choked back tears.

XIX

I book my next client, Handstandbuck, for 12:30, which is forty minutes from now. He's this middle-aged man who works at Scotiabank. He prefers twinks, he says, and has a deep appreciation for "Native Americans." He really admires our traditions and thinks our culture is beautiful. I text him: "Like me?" and he sends me a winky emoji. He has a wife and two kids but secretly wants to sleep with men. That's where I come in. He'll take his lunch at 12:30, go to the office bathroom, turn on his iPhone, and Skype with me for thirty minutes until he comes all over the bathroom stall. He's an easy one since he doesn't yet know what he wants; a flash of skin and some dirty talk usually gets him off. He's a quick twenty bones.

But forty minutes? That's a long time to wait and I'm already feeling horny again.

I play with my hair to make myself feel good, it reminds me of how it felt when my kokum would run her rough hands from my widow's peak to my crown. There's this young new-age couple who live above me and I'm not sure if it's the banging of their washing machine or if it's they themselves who are banging—but there are these loud frequent noises they make, like drumbeats, that remind me of my kokum. Sometimes I'll sit against the wall to feel the vibrations and smoke a cigarette, thinking the tobacco is an offering that filters through me. My landlord says I'm not supposed to smoke in the building but I really don't give a fuck, I think I've every right to destroy my body, to be ceremonial on settler land.

An elder told me once that I could heal myself of my drinking habits if I went to a sweat lodge. He said that I'd have to wear something modest. I planned to go with my kokum, who was going to wear a long skirt adorned with ribbons that she had made. I loved it so much that I asked if she could make me one. She smiled, sent me home with a slab of bannock, and when I returned the next day, she had sewn me one just like hers. But when we arrived at the sweat lodge, the elder wouldn't let me in. "Modesty," he repeated, "is key." My skirt apparently did not meet his ceremonial expectations; he told me to take it off and put on a pair of XXL Adidas shorts he had, or to return at another date in proper attire. While my kokum argued with him in Cree, I flipped him off and stormed back to the van. It turns out that tradition is an NDN's saving grace, but it's a medicine reserved only for certain members of the reservation, and not for self-ordained Injun glitter princesses like me. This tradition repeats throughout my life: I'm expected to chop wood for ceremonies rather than knead fry-bread, learn how to hunt with my uncles rather than knit with my aunties, perform the Fancy Feather dance when I really want to do the Jingle Dress dance. "Man up" was the mantra of my childhood and teenage years, because the dick between my legs wasn't enough proof of ownership of NDN manhood. There are a million parts of me that don't add up, a million parts of me that signal immodesty. When I think of masculinity, I think of femininity.

Everything's finished in beauty.

I used to dream about a dress that had the colours of the medicine wheel: black, white, yellow, and red. I finally made one from some clearance clothes I found at the Sally Ann: I ripped out the stitches down to the original panels, cut out pieces from a McCall's pattern I found at Value Village, and restitched them back into a dress that drapes over my body like a second skin. I hole-punched recycled soup can lids and sewed them to the dress instead of bells. It jingles gloriously when I dance around my living room in it. The dress is lovely and makes me feel like an NDN Sally Finkelstein.

Since I would never have been allowed this dress on the rez, I felt rebellious in my creation of it. I had to make my own. And to really put the cherry on top, I added a "modest" slit up the leg à la Angelina Jolie.

I am my own best medicine.

XX

Truth be told, I did need a lot of healing throughout my teen years. I am The Vacuum for a reason; drinking became a problem for me early on. I loved how alcohol made me feel; it gave me confidence, courage, and when I was drinking was the only time I could love and be loved. Desperate drunk boys flocked to me like leeches to a pickerel. In their blacked-out haze they'd tell me almost anything for a blowjob, and I'd do them. I loved it when they said, "I love you, Jonny, I do," like a personal mantra that would make them come harder. They wouldn't get me off, but I found my own sustenance from making straight NDN boys love me like their pow wow trail hookups. They'd cuddle me at night and then kick me out in the morning, denying any closeness and blaming it all on the drink. Truth be told, I think I was more a leech than they were. I loved the burning hot flesh of brown skin turning red from tension and friction. I loved seeing the blood throb in their veins, popping like earthworms on their forearms and wrists—blood that said I'm surviving and you can too. Like the leech, I too felt like a hermaphrodite: part boy, part girl, and always needed by hunters and fishermen. And I always left a red mark on their bodies somewhere, as if to say: I was here.

Plus, leeches are medicine, didn't you know?

After a while, these black-out hookups became the norm for me, and I, The Vacuum, was expected to perform as the drunkest one at the party. The boys would feed me shots and the girls would try to fight me through the night. It was a dysfunctional loop of love and hate. Such is NDN life. My jaw would often be sore, stretched too much from fingers and cock, and my ass would bottom out from these random hookups. Sex, for me, just became an expectation of every rez party.

Love-making was a term that wasn't part of my vocabulary. I learned to be sexy and have sex thanks to alcohol. I lost my virginity at fourteen to a boy whose name I can't even remember. In fact, all of my sexual experiences are similar: I rarely, if ever, had sober sex.

I remember one night regaining consciousness at a house party, in a bed that smelled of piss and Labatt Blue, while a man stood over me. I was on my back, buck-naked, my neck curved over the side of the bed and my eyes staring up at this man's penis that was lacerating my tonsils. The next morning I woke up with a patch of semen cemented on my chest. I was like a map of DNA, a living river, you could read my body like a book and pinpoint where you'd been and where you would want to go.

My shirt was nowhere to be seen, nor was he, but his wallet was, so I took forty dollars and also stole a sweater from the mound of clothes on the floor. I never did find out who he was, never really cared. But he was my first in-person client.

I was sixteen.

XXI

I was eighteen the first time I realized I was a drunken NDN. The Peguis Hotel and Casino had just opened and everyone on the rez decided to throw a big party there, especially since almost all of us had been recently hired, including me. The hotel manager, who was a newish client of mine, got me in as a dishwasher. The pay was shitty, but I didn't really do it for the money, it was more so that I could pass out my number and screenname to any potential new customers I met, of which there were plenty. Gay men have this weird way of recognizing each other, like facial recognition software or some cyborg skill from *The Terminator*. It's not gaydar, but more like a secret sign written on the face. My kokum says the eyes never age or lie, and I found out that a gay man's eyes always give him away. Sometimes it's written in the cheekbones, other times it's written in the walk, but it always hangs like a veil over their eyes.

There was this older gentleman, grey hair, great build, and a real catamite ass that Zeus himself would have smote. Hell if I remember his name, but I remember his eyes—a powder blue speckled with light grey, like the stones that glittered at the bottom of the Peguis rapids in the middle of July. We ran into each other at the casino party while everyone was in a stupor, even my kokum was sipping and jigging to Conway Twitty. He cracked us a couple beers from his cooler full of Labatt Lites and we drank on the VLT stools while Lobstermania spun behind us in a haze of colours and bright lights. As the beers set in, we both got a little friskier. I found his hand on my knee. We had both read the queerness in each other's eyes. Both wanted a little more. Both a little thirstier. Our fingers pruned from spilled beer. The tips of his ears reddening. My cheeks heating up. Pupils dilating. Stone iris. Flared nostrils. Deep smile lines. Pores open and sweating.

I awoke in the hospital the next morning, with five stitches that haphazardly ran down from the nape of my neck to the centre of my back, skin glue on my nose, my arms and shoulders darkened with bruises. I was groggy for two whole days afterwards—I never found out exactly what happened. All I know is that no hangover had ever incapacitated me like that before. The nurse told me the police brought me in for falling through a lobby window. She asked me if I had any drinks and I could only reply, "I think so." I was crying and the nurse tried comforting me. I asked if I was being charged. Where were the police? Was I going to jail? I cried into her scrubs and asked to call my mom. When Mom picked up the phone and I explained what had happened, she only said, "You're a real NDN now," and hung up.

I started weeping profusely.

Later that night, I was allowed to go home. The nurse dug into her purse and snuck me a twenty-dollar bill for a cab. She hugged me and said young boys like me shouldn't be drinking as much as I was. Bless her white heart, I said to myself, she didn't know that getting a cab to go to the rez at night was damn near impossible. Nor did she know that we used depressants to offset our deep depression. I'd have better luck going home in a police car, or better yet being sent to the drunk tank. I took the twenty and thanked her. I hobbled to my feet and realized that my keys, my wallet, my phone, all of it was gone.

There were rips down the back of my shirt from where the glass cut me. I didn't even try to get a cab; I pocketed the twenty and walked the hour-long trek in between bouts of near unconsciousness.

I remember snippets of my walk home. The howls of coyotes along the backroads, and gusts of wind that burnt my face. The night sky looking like soot and a blood-orange supermoon hung above me. Lights flying across the sky like a dollar-store sparkler; I thought it was aliens. The black-beaded eye of a rez dog glistening from a ditch; it sounded like it was ripping apart a jackrabbit. An ATV tearing by me, spitting gravel into the air. Ravens cawing from atop evergreens. The smells of smoke and sage.

As I finally rounded the corner of my house, the sun was rising and the sky was a blend of custard and corn-kernel yellows. The entire rez was silent, everyone either asleep or passed out, more likely the latter. A few fires still crackled and the air was full of thick, sweet smoke. My feet were bruised from the gravel road and prickled with pain. Inside my house, I fell asleep on the couch, crying for my mom.

I didn't fully sober up until two days later when Mom, Kokum, and Roger came back from their own bender. Mom gasped when she saw me and scooped me into her arms. She smelled like a stale Chanel knock-off and her sweat tasted like beer. Her beaded teal earrings caught my hair, but I let her hold me and cry even if it hurt me to do so. "M'boy, my sweet boy, kisâkihitin, kisâkihitin."

I told myself then and there that I'd quit the firewater. I learned later that the dazzler in the sky wasn't a UFO, it was a meteor shower named the Perseids. My kokum told me it was a lesson to be learned and that the stitches on my back was Nanaboozhoo's handprint. She said those meteors haven't been seen in 133 years and were a part of this comet called Swift-Tuttle. When I Googled "Perseid" later, I discovered that it is the "single most dangerous object known to humanity." Now, when I think back on that night, I still see that beady black rez-dog eye and the mane of dust that looked like Sasquatch on the backroads.

"I can be this too," I tell myself. "I can be this too."

When I look in the mirror at the handprint on my back, I see the same lifelines on it that are on my palm: a radiant 'M' that if twisted, spells Me. Seeing the scar and remembering the shreds of skin that inlet into my body, I am reminded that I can die here too.

There are times when you have to scare yourself to find yourself.

XXII

I told Tias about that night a few weeks afterwards. He came over while my mom was at bingo and my kokum was in Winnipeg for the weekend. My body was shaking involuntarily as I recalled the story for him. I had to sit down and he took me to my room which was less an Ikea showroom and more a hand-me-down mattress without a boxspring on the floor and a hamper for a dresser. My saving grace was my box TV and our pirated satellite. He brought me a cold cloth and laid it on my forehead and told me everything was going to be okay. I asked him if he could hold me and say that. He did.

After a few minutes, he took my hand in his and we laid our legs over top each other like a wishbone. We both stayed there looking at each other, not saying a word, sweat forming on our brows in the dry heat of August. I moved the cloth so it draped over both of us and we slid our heads that much closer. The tips of our noses touched and we left them there, puckering for a kunik.

We clasped one another like a zipper. The cloth blocked out all light and we lay side by side in darkness. I felt the heat of his breath on my cupid's bow. We slid off our jeans and raised our T-shirts to press our bodies closer, our nipples kissing too. Our breaths grew heavy. His thighs were bony and my clavicle dug into his, but it was the most comfortable I'd been in a long time.

After our bodies were drenched in sweat, we pulled off the cloth and laughed. He stared at me for a long time. I saw new parts of his body I'd never seen before: a chickenpox scar on his cheek, the width of his bottom lip. We both knew what the other was feeling.

Instead of saying we liked or loved each other, we just lay there on our backs, our brown skin shiny in the rosy light that poured in from the evening sun. We surveyed each other's body: him seeing the scar above my clavicle from when I fell down the stairs as a kid, and me seeing the patch of hair missing from his scalp. I knew then that I loved him.

Funny how an NDN "love you" sounds more like, "I'm in pain with you."

XXIII

Lucia died when I was twelve. Tias asked her, meaning me, if we could meet up, and I, thinking maybe I was girl-boy enough to elude his anxieties, said yes. We went to the Pine Cone Dairy Bar and I wondered what he was expecting. I spotted him in the back corner of the restaurant. He was wearing an Iron Maiden T-shirt and brown khaki shorts. His black hair was ruffled into a mess and faux-hawked. His shoes were muddy Nikes—basic, I thought, but cute nonetheless. We went to the same school but we hadn't ever talked. Lord knows why, we were both at the bottom of the school's popularity spectrum. He stuck to art classes and liked to paint while I was more interested in learning how to cook apple crisp in home ec and smoking on the steps of the Holy Eucharist church with the "Bad Girls." They used to hate being called the Bad Girls. Really, all we did was refashion cigarettes from the butts of others and make each other laugh. We had nowhere to go, no one to turn to, so we stuck to ourselves. "Donna Summer," I told them, "man, she's a bad-ass-bad-girl." *Bad Girls* was the first CD I ever saved up enough to buy, and I worshipped it like nobody's business. The girls didn't care for it, but I thought, hell yeah, I'm a bad girl.

Sitting on those church steps, I would look up at the porcelain-skinned man crucified over the main door and would think of the photos my kokum showed me of lynched NDNs hanging from trees. I had no concept of their being dead, I just thought they were these beautifully arranged, angelic, aerial dancers serving face and body from these great oaks like real children of the forest. I wanted to be that too, so I would vogue on the church's front lawn and lock my eyes with christ's as Donna Summer moaned and came into my headphones.

At the Dairy Bar, I let Tias sit there by himself for a while, awkwardly surveying the room for a hypersexual, blessedly-breasted, plastically-altered, red-headed Russian glamazon named Lucia. His defeated look was a sad sight, but I took some joy in watching him writhe—his face was flushed a dusky pink that complemented his skin tone well. Tias has always been so wondrously pained; it would become something I'd learn to love. Pain only intensifies the real emotions worth feeling; hell, every NDN knows a thing or two about intensity.

After I had taken enough pleasure watching him bottle up his fantasies and agonize over the fact that he'd be returning home a virgin, I approached his table.

"Stood up, 'er what?"

"What?"

"You're Mathias, eh? We go to the same school, y'know?"

"Yeah, I thought I recognized you. You're the queer in Ms Blackbird's class?"

"Yeah, man, that's me."

I sat down and asked him who he was waiting for. I looked at the hairs on his sandy brown arms as I listened to him tell me about the girl he met online. He told me that he got money for his date by stealing from his mom's bingo change. We started talking and soon learned that both of us were broke as hell—heck, I paid for my sundae with rolled coin—but we had fantasies, dreams, and big imaginations that would last us through the rez and beyond. We both wanted houses like the ones on *MTV Cribs* and we idolized Ed the Sock. Looking back, I take a little pride in knowing that I was Tias's first lesson on the difference between fantasy and reality—he wished for a Russian princess and instead got the reservation's only gay NDN.

The sun was beginning to set when we finally left the Dairy Bar and we were both late for dinner. We chalked it up to our parents' most infamous excuse: we were running on NDN time. We laughed but knew this wouldn't do, we knew full well the lickin that awaited us at home. We walked together down the backroads, both a little scared of the bears and coyotes that lurked in the bush. We had our keys interlinked between our fingers and our hands curled into hard fists in case anything, or anyone, jumped out at us. We walked so close to each other that the hard bone of our middle fingers continually knocked together. Our boniness hurt but neither of us broke our pace—the friction of our raw knuckles banging together was oddly comforting.

As we neared our homes, Logan and his cousins passed by us on their four-wheelers. Tias panicked and stopped in his tracks. They often beat up Tias, so he was used to trying to become invisible in their presence. The boys spun around and drove up behind us.

"Hey, gayboys," one of them yelled.

"Tias, is this your new girlfriend?" another asked.

"Two little faggots, sitting in a tree," Logan laughed.

"He's not—" Tias started.

"We're just friends, Logan, heck, obsessed much?" I said.

The boys circled their four-wheelers around us and stood up on their seats with their arms crossed.

"K-I-S-S-I-N-G," Logan continued.

"I'm not—"

"Hey, gayboys."

"H-I-V and A-I-D."

"There's an S in there too, Logan, at least get it right," I said.

Logan got red in the face and nodded to the other boys, who were now surrounding us. Tias crouched down with his head between his knees, repeatedly saying the word "No." The boys all grinned and unzipped their pants.

"Hey Hoover," Logan exclaimed, "here's some cock for you." And then each boy pulled out their floppy penises and urinated all over me. My clothes were soaked and my hair was shiny with piss.

"Hey Tias, if he ain't your girlfriend then piss on him too, eh?" Logan said.

Tias was still crouching behind me, his eyes closed. Logan and his posse, waiting for Tias to join in on their golden shower, crossed their arms and waited. One of Logan's friends slapped his fist against his palm. Tias opened his eyes and I held his gaze as he slowly stood up. His hands were shaking as he slowly undid his zipper. I closed my eyes and nodded. The warmth of his urine splashing on my shirt startled me. When I opened my eyes, he was crying. His limp penis hung and the last few drops of piss leaked from his fingers. His eyes were sunk deep in his head and his arms were wrapped around his waist. His entire body read regret, but even then, I thought, no boy has ever looked so goddamned precious.

XXIV

Tias and I used to hustle Mush when we were kids. I liked my mushom, he was a gentle, soft-spoken man who loved Werther's caramels and Budweiser. He used to buy me party-sized chocolate bars, like those Jumbo Mr. Bigs that were twice the size of your head. He wasn't NDN like us, but Kokum insisted we call him Mushom. His real name was Pierre LeClerc and he was the luckiest, and only, môniyâw on the reservation. He won $100,000 on a scratch ticket when he was in his thirties and from then on out he became popular among the family and all the rez girls. He bought my mom a used Cadillac Seville and that forced her to called him Mush—half liking him, half detesting him. He used the remainder of his winnings to buy a gas station that was quite successful while he was alive. He liked to give all the NDN kids a piece of candy whenever they visited, and overloaded their bags with Twizzlers and Pop-Rocks on Halloween. He was a dandy fellow.

But there were better ways to get money from him than by simply asking. Sure, if you asked kindly enough, he'd throw you a few dollars, maybe ten bones if you were really lucky, and then shame you for it when he was on his benders. If there's one rule I've learned from hustling, it's never to put yourself into a situation where you owe somebody—always leave your clients owing you. Though, if you were patient enough, you could swindle forty to fifty bones from Mush by waiting for him to pass out and collecting all his empties. His house would be littered with aluminum: cans in his sink, cans in his bed, cans in the pockets of his coat, crumpled in his war chest. Tias and I used to wait at his place and listen to him and Kokum tell us stories about the good ol' days which would usually erupt into an argument about who had it worse—that's the thing about old folks, they think life is a competition of scars and suffering.

When Mush passed out and Kokum kept herself busy calling everyone she knew on the phone, Tias and I would begin collecting cans like the hermit crabs that cleaned the aquariums in those city pet stores. After we had loaded up two recycle bags' worth, we'd take them to the vendor and exchange them for forty dollars. After we split the cash, we'd go to Mush's gas station and load up on all types of candy: gummies, chocolates, peppermints, Eskimo Pie, and everyone's personal favourite, Nestle Redskins. Usually, if we didn't have enough for what we wanted, one of us would distract Mush's cashier and the other would load candy into their coat.

With what little money we had left, we'd buy a few cigarettes from the junior high chumps who stole them from their moms. They actually made decent money by selling cigarettes for a dollar. Then we'd take our goods back home to gorge on the candy as we watched *Ren and Stimpy* late into the night. High on sugar, we'd then smoke the cigarettes to give ourselves a head rush and walk around the room light-headed and dizzy—it was the closest we could get to being fucked up as ten-year-olds. Sometimes we would take turns puffing on Kokum's inhaler too, until she caught on and gave us both a damn good slap with her wooden spoon. That's how we thought it was, that being drunk and high were natural processes to growing up.

There were times, if I looked pitiful enough, like a brown-skin

Annie singing "It's a Hard Knock Life" sad, that my kokum would let Tias stay over on weekends. We would both sleep upstairs in my uncle's old bedroom, but before we did we'd argue about who got to sleep against the wall, which was always way cooler. To beat the heat, we'd jack the small fan from my kokum's bedroom and put it in ours, which also helped to drown out the clanging of their bottles downstairs—it disrupted our watching of *Boy Meets World*. While Tias raved over how beautiful Topanga was, I swooned over Shawn. And the real name of the actor who played him was so erotically charged for me: Rider Strong. I used to whisper it to myself to fall asleep because I liked the way it sounded when I inserted a heavy breath into the spaces between its syllables. I would lay my tongue down on the bottom of my mouth and let the air vibrate and stimulate them: "Riiide," "der," "Strawwng." A good name makes the perfect sex toy.

Sometimes there would be a party downstairs, and we'd sneak down and watch my kokum, Mush, my mother, my aunts and uncles, cousins, the gas station employees, a tribal officer, and a cavalcade of brown-skins dance around to Loretta Lynn. As Loretta wailed about her man not coming home a-drinking, I would tiptoe into the room and say goodnight to everyone. Funny, the people who loved me the most could only tell me so between two and three in the morning. Then, while they professed their love and pride for me, I'd sneak a couple beers into the pockets of my sweatpants. Back upstairs, Tias and I would crack them open and pretend we thought they tasted good.

"Damn good beer, eh?" Tias said on one such night.

"I've had better, you know?" I replied.

"No, that's the name," he said. "Damn Good Beer, Minhas Creek—wonder where the Damn Good Chips are?"

We buckled with a laugh that ran so deeply through our bodies that our abs hurt afterwards. Then we flipped through the late-night channels, mostly old white women trying to sell patches for varicose veins and Chyna wrestling in the WWF, until we settled on the Showcase Channel and watched a show called *KinK*. There was a drag queen who was putting on makeup and kaikaiing with another queen. The taller of the two backed the other against the wall, slid her hand up the other's thigh, and slowly raised her dress, revealing the garters underneath. The shorter one then pulled the other's hands up against her body and wrapped her legs around her. We were both mesmerized.

Afterwards, while we both tried to sleep, Tias asked me if I thought that scene looked like fun. I giggled and said yeah. He laughed, but then he slid closer to me and I felt his hand on my leg. I rolled onto his chest and spread both of my legs over his torso. We started giggling, our bodies vibrating with each other's. It felt like we were a guitar and our lungs and esophagus were being strummed like strings. Fitting, I thought, as we made our own music and let our limbs dance their own ballet without ever moving. Downstairs, Loretta howled in the background that the squaw was on the warpath tonight. We fell asleep like buttons in buttonholes.

The next morning, when the sun was rising, my mom came into our room and nudged my shoulder.

"The heck you doing, boy?"

She put her arms under my pits and raised me up. I wrapped my arms and legs around her and breathed her in, the smoke, the booze, the sweat and tears that made up her perfume. She rubbed the wetness from my eyes, which she called sleepies, and kissed my cheek. I opened my eyes wider and saw a patch of blood on her dry lips, and the black mascara streaming down her face. Even in my half-asleep state, I was both afraid and concerned.

"What happened?" I asked.

"M'boy," she said, pulling my face against her breast and starting to cry. "I'm not the drink, I swear, okay? I'm not the drink."

She put me back into bed beside Tias, who was still asleep, and covered us with a blanket. She kissed us both on the forehead and said, "My boys, kisâkihitin."

I could hear Roger calling her from downstairs, his shout sounding more like the pitiful welp of a dog licking its wounds after a fight.

"Mom?" I said. "Can you lay with me until I fall asleep?"

She smiled and crawled in between Tias and me, pulling us tight against her body. Tias was stirring now, and both of us nuzzled our sleepy heads against her, until her heartbeat lulled us back to sleep. When we finally woke up later, we discovered that one of us had pissed the bed.

We never found out who.

XXV

It was midnight and I had just finished with my seventh client of the day. Some guy named TimOTron cheated me out of ten bucks because he wanted Masc4Masc. My body was stinging and my penis sore from the constant friction. Tired as I was, I was also excited that I had made one-fifty in a couple of hours; I really couldn't complain. If I were eager enough, I could wait a few more hours and get my European clients who were six hours ahead; they'd be finishing their work day soon and coming home horny as hell. But my body was saying I needed a break so I lit a butt and sat against the window ledge in my bathroom. I wanted to talk to the pigeon, have him listen to me, but he was asleep, tucked beneath a heap of garbage. I checked my phone to see if Tias had messaged me. The little box for "Message Sent" was grey, indicating his phone had received the message but he hadn't read it yet. Typical, I said, and sighed when I saw him posting memes on Facebook. I wondered what he was doing over at his mom's right then. I wondered, was he watching *The Walking Dead*? Was he touching himself? Was he thinking of me? Or was he texting her again?

Hungry, I decided to walk the few blocks over to 7-11 to spend a few of my hard-earned dollars and get a Big Bite. The place actually made half decent hot dogs and they were cheap to boot. Once, before I set the rule of never meeting clients in person, I agreed to go out with this guy, corkdub78, who was some thirty-something mechanic at Crappy Tire. He said he was straight but sort of a "tranny chaser"; I told him I was Two-Spirit, not transgender, and that tranny was an out-of-date word. When he looked puzzled, I told him, okay, well, if you popped my hood you'd find that I'm a machine too. He didn't understand. Score one for The Vacuum.

He took me to a fancy dinner at The Keg where the minimum cost for a meal was fifty dollars. I suggested we split a plate and he looked at me like I was the cheapest fuck he'd ever met. If life were a game of Monopoly, my mother would be the banker. She was as economical as they came; she could turn seven dollars into a meal for eight. A rule of thumb, she told me once, was to never put myself into a position where I would owe someone—"Too much power," she said. "You'll pay it over threefold." So I never let anyone pay for my meals, let alone a date. A slice of overcooked steak and a scoop of mashed potatoes doesn't buy me. I always split the bill, but if you really wanted to be strategic, especially if you liked the guy, you could take control and pay for the entire meal yourself—make them owe you.

I convinced corkdub78 that I wasn't that hungry and that we should split a main course and then grab a coffee afterwards. He agreed and we shared a sirloin steak and baked potato. I ate slowly and took little bites, thinking I would make it last longer. But to be honest, the steak sucked and the potato was undercooked.

But before I knew it my fat fuck companion had scarfed down every bit left on the plate. All I had eaten was a few slices of meat and a few bites of potato. To hell with this, I thought, so I grabbed my coat and excused myself for the bathroom. The guy wasn't all that bright, christ, he didn't even ask why I needed my coat to take a leak. I slipped out the patio door and dine-and-dashed his ass so hard. Afterwards,

I hit up McDonald's and devoured two Junior Chickens. That's the problem with white guys, they think they can impress you with fancy meals and expense accounts if you let them. I really don't give a shit about how much money you make or how many bathrooms your condo has. If you want to impress a neechi, you need to take them out to an Applebee's or Montana's or even Foody Goody's Chinese Buffet and let them enjoy a smorgasbord of food for $12.99. And if you really want to impress them you could swing by a Co-Op and split a carton of white mini-donuts. No Cree boy gives a rat's ass for escargot or lobster tails. Shit's nasty.

Back at the 7-11, I bought two Big Bites, a chocolate milk, and a pack of cigarettes, and sat on the curb outside eating. The streets of Portage were lively with noise: cars thumping in potholes, snippets of hip hop from a balcony across the street, the clang of bells from the Asian Food Market, the low thrum of a motorbike, a bottle smashing in the distance.

"Can't you read?" a voice shouted from behind me. "No loitering!"

I brushed the man off with my hand and felt him shove a corn broom against my back.

"Goddamn Natives, always sitting around here. Hurry up and leave before I call the cops." The store manager hit me with his broom again and held it there; the bristles dug into my back. It felt kind of exciting. I pushed back against the bristles. It felt good to be hurt like that. He pushed harder and knocked me off the curb. My milk slipped out of my hand and spilled down my shirt, pooling between my legs and seeping beneath the curb. I wondered how many bugs would drown and die down there.

"That's it, I'm calling the cops," he said. "Damn drunken kids."

I lay down on the sidewalk and spread my arms and legs like a starfish. I wondered if some alien up above was looking down at me thinking I was a constellation.

"Final warning," he said.

I lit a cigarette and puffed on it without any hands. Smoke slithered out of my nostrils. I winked at him. "You know," I stated between puffs, "this *is* my land, you ingrate."

"*Your* land?" he said. "Who the hell do you think you are, you punk? I pay the fucking tax here, the tax that pays for your welfare, you good-for-nothing—" He stormed off back into Sev as the ashes from my cigarette began to drop on me. They burned a little, singeing what little hair I had on my face—"Muskrat hair," Tłas always said. "The blessing of being a Nate is that we only need to buy one razor per year."

I sat up and saw the manager talking animatedly on his landline, staring in my direction. I got up and threw my hood on. Good luck finding me, there are a million loitering NDNs in Winnipeg tonight.

There's something quintessential about being me and walking at night. Finishing a seven-hour wank session, feeling exhausted, overworked, burnt out, underpaid, sad, hungry, lonely, nostalgic, and strangely beautiful during a one a.m. Sev-run. I calculated that it took me two hundred steps to walk the block back to my apartment. On the front steps of my building, I lit another cigarette. I thought, if it takes two hundred steps to walk a block, then there are two thousand steps in a mile. I wondered, if I walked 600,000 steps, if they'd call me Navajo and let me be a real NDN?

An elderly woman shouted out her window that if I didn't get up and go, she'd call the cops. Cops, I thought, everyone's always threatening me with cops. I waved my keycard at her and rolled my eyes. She huffed and closed her window. I could still feel her eyes watching me from behind the blinds. I wondered who she thought I was. Do people think I'm another ghost on the boulevard? Am I a vanishing NDN? If I disappeared, would they look for me like they did that woman, Thelma Krull? Would they rally behind my death like they did for that dead lion, Cecil? Nah, I thought. I'd become another name on the registry. My head felt light but my chest felt heavy.

I wished Tias would come over.

XXVI

When I got back to my apartment, I threw myself onto the couch. It was one of those brown micro-suede plush couches with maroon-coloured roses blooming on the fabric. It was my kokum's old couch and still smelled of her: flour, cigarettes, and makeup. I used to love watching her put on her makeup. I'd sit beside her and gawk into the handheld mirror she used to apply her eyeshadow. My kokum only got dolled up on rare occasions, which were mostly bingo nights and funerals. I always find it mesmerizing to watch a woman put on her face: the soft stroke of the brush that sends translucent powder flying into the air; the steady hand necessary to blend shadows and wing an eye.

She always took her time, routinely stopping to puff on a cigarette and flip through the TV channels to find a wrestling match. My kokum had an unparalleled love for Bret "The Hitman" Hart. I adored that about her, the fact that the tiniest woman you'd ever meet would be screaming at the top of her lungs for the Hitman to "finish him off with a Sharpshooter." She'd stomp her feet when he lost and all of the pictures on her walls would rattle—the various school portraits of her children and grandchildren. Mine was in the top left-hand corner, I'm wearing a wool sweater and my hair is slicked back into two braids. I'm sitting in front of a bookcase, which my family said made me look smart. I wonder, what would they think if I told them I jacked off on cam to pay my rent and talked to pigeons in my spare time? But Kokum loved that photo and put it in her fanciest gold frame. And in front of it she had tucked a tiny Polaroid of the two of us laughing, our faces smudged with lipstick. In the picture we are leaning against each other on the couch; her frizzy hair blends into my shaggy braids and the points of our noses exactly match. There is a large red kiss-print on my forehead. That was the first time I ever wore makeup. She would apply her powders and lotions to my face with such grace and softness that I would fall asleep, smelling of talc and lilac. She would push back my hair with her hand and tickle my widow's peak with her fingers, applying concealer to the scar there. I like thinking that she is impressed on my forehead even now—that the stories in her body are written on mine.

I was feeling nostalgic, like every other NDN at two a.m., so I called up Tias. He answered, half groggy, half annoyed, whispering a faint "Hello?" into the receiver.

"Hey," I said, "you still got that Hamburger Helper?"

XXVII

I made my way down to Tias's house and snuck in through his window. We were both masters at popping out window screens without breaking them. See, if you slide a butter knife in between the screen and the window frame and then wiggle it back and forth, you can pop out the bottom plugs that click it into place; from there on, you can push it in with your thumbs. In fact, NDNs have hacked a million tools out of everyday objects. You can use a coat hanger as a toaster if you bend it into a 'V' and place it on top of an element. It makes some damn good NDN toast.

I crawled in through the window and fell on top of Tias on the bed. "You awake?" I jokingly asked and he nudged me in the ribs. His skin was a dusky hue in the pale luminescent light. I saw he was reading some book by Charles Dickens.

"What's that about?" I asked, rubbing the wrinkled spine of the book.

"You know that Christmas movie about Donald Duck and those three ghosts?"

I nodded.

"It's that, but you know, not Disney. You wouldn't like it."

Feeling insulted, I dug around his room as he kept reading. There was a copy of *Ariel* on the floor, open to a story titled "Daddy." I wondered if he had a fetish for older men? I turned my attention to his closet; there were crumpled-up jeans, a few shirts, these *Redwall* books with mice fighting other mice on the cover, and a bundle of fabric tied together with elastics. I untied it and found this old rabbit plush toy wrapped up inside it. It had a brown body with a white belly and blue eyes that were hot-glued onto its head. Its left ear had been torn off and was held in place with a pin.

"I've had him pretty much all my life," Tias said. "Floppy Ears. My grandpa gave him to me when I was a boy, well, I mean, one of my foster grandpas, not my biological. He was this old Polish man, survived the war and everything, a real hard ass."

"This guy is sure beat up, eh?" I laughed.

"Heck, that ain't even half of it."

"What do you mean?"

"Throw him here."

I tossed it over to him and he pulled his neck tight. "See these stitches? He had his head ripped off from one of my first foster placements. I lived on this farm with a Ukrainian family just a few miles outside of the rez. They raised cattle and our neighbour had an ostrich farm. I used to play with them all the time and I'd bring Flop. We'd go up to their pens and feed them seeds. When I teased them they'd ruffle their feathers and start running in circles. Then one time one of those goddamn ostriches stretched his long-ass neck out and plucked Flop straight from my hands. He ran around the pen and all the other birds nipped at him. And I guess these two birds got into a fight over Flop—they ripped his head clean off. My foster mom later went and collected his head, body, and his gutted innards. She stitched him back up for me. I wasn't allowed near the birds after that."

I laughed. "That's crazy. That's some Looney Toons realness."
Tias sat quietly and cradled his plush.

"Sorry, Tias," I said after a few moments of silence. "Shit's rough.
But hey, you still got this little guy."

"Yeah," he said, "little guy's the toughest sonuva I've ever met.
Been through hell and back and he's still here. He's a fucking mess."
He laughed. "But every mess on his body has a funny story behind it."

I climbed into bed beside him, nuzzled my head between his
armpit and pectoral. He wasn't wearing deodorant, but I kind of liked
his stink, it was one of his sexiest attributes. I laid my left arm and leg
over his body and he rested his chin on my forehead.

"Oh yeah?" I said. "You gotta tell me sometime—"

"Little by little," he interjected. "Little. By. Little."

As we began to feel sleepy, I thought about the Dickens book he
was reading. He was right, I didn't care for it but that doesn't mean I
hadn't read it. I think Ebenezer and I had a lot in common: we both
liked money and to screw. And weren't we both haunted by ghosts?

"Tell me one?" I whispered to Tias.

"Okay," he yawned, "but I don't know where to begin."

"To begin with," I suggested.

"Yeah?"

"You got an ass laden with wood."

"Ekosi," he laughed.

"You don't say," I replied, in between kisses knitted with girlish
laughter.

XXVIII

I never cried when my kokum died—I reserved my energy for telling stories and making everybody around me laugh. My voice, my body, my life—every piece of me is a bundle of medicine that gives and burns and smudges. When she died, she was wearing a blue and white hospital gown with pale blue diamonds patterned on it. I had watched those diamonds rise and fall with every one of her breaths for twelve hours straight as she lay unconscious in a hospital bed, until they finally stopped. I was alone with her when she died; only her and me at three in the morning. When her bloated belly stopped filling with breath, I rubbed it and felt it gurgle. My kokum taught me long ago when my aunty died, that we need to rub the breath out of the belly of the dead.

"It's to help them on their way," she said. "That's what us women do—we help them on their way back home."

So I rubbed my grandma's belly and put my ear to her mouth. Then I crawled onto the bed beside her and laid my head on her breast. I maneuvered one of her arms around me and the other hand atop my head. My favourite feeling in the world was when she clawed my hair with her fingers to put me to sleep. Her hand fit perfectly on my head like a bird sitting atop a ledge. We lay like this for a bit—I didn't tell the nurse she had stopped breathing and because we had unhooked her from the machines, they didn't know she had died. I slipped her monitor off her finger and pressed it onto mine. I wanted a few minutes like this, just us.

The nurses were busybodies, I could hear them scurrying about in rooms adjacent to ours. They were telling jokes and laughing. Their happiness pissed me off. Stop fucking laughing, I thought, my kokum's lying here dead. I drowned them out with a prayer. I told Manito I love him still. I told the ghosts that permeated our room that maybe I'm ready too, you know? Maybe I'm ready to go; itsokayitsokayit- sokay. I laid there not moving, trying desperately to sleep, trying my hardest to will myself into death. I closed my eyes and said here it comes, it's coming, it's here. And when I could open them again, I wondered what was wrong with me; why not now? Wasn't the lifeline in my palm broken too?

When a nurse eventually came into the room and discovered that my kokum had passed, she asked me if I was okay. By then the tears had already crusted in the corner of my eyes. "Of course," I replied. I didn't tell her that I thought something inside me was dead too; didn't tell her that something inside me had been broken for years, if not centuries.

She wrote up a report and closed my kokum's eyes, then walked out of the room and summoned a doctor. In the room beside us, another nurse was still laughing.

Sometimes I don't like how life goes on.

And sometimes I don't think it should.

XXVIX

My head is the most sensual area on my body. When someone runs their hands through my hair and gently applies pressure on my temples, I can fall asleep on a dime. My mom and kokum used to put me to sleep this way when I was a kid; they'd run their fingers like a rake from the top of my forehead down to the nape of my neck.

After my kokum died, I spent a lot of time alone. It was Tias who got me through the whole ordeal. He came over every day and talked with me. If I was in bed he'd sit on top of the sheets beside me. Hell, he even sat beside me while I wallowed in the tub. And I don't even remember what it was we talked about, except that sometimes he'd tell me stories of his foster dad as if he were some benevolent white christ figure. But the way he told stories was so sincere that I couldn't help but become enamoured. That was when I learned just how much power there is in stories—they can transform an alcoholic, child-beating sonuva into a saintly man who loves and gives annually to Unicef. I don't know what it was that Tias loved about that man, but he loved him nonetheless. I had to respect him for that.

He'd often ask about my dad and I'd never have much of a reply except for the automated response I'd memorized, the "I was two years old and he died in a rez fire, it was real tragic" spiel. Truth is, I never knew my father. When he died in the fire a few years after he left us, Mom said he was messing around with some slooze named Pauline because he couldn't handle being a dad. I wondered if she blamed me for taking away the great love of her life. She told me about how

great of a pow wow dancer he was. He used to wear red and black ribbons and was the highlight of every Men's Traditional Dance on the
pow wow trail. Mom said he moved like a brutish bison, and how his
muscles would glisten in the afternoon sun. That, and I overheard her
once saying that he was hung like a bull too. I guess that trait skipped
a generation.

I have a few photos of him that I found in my kokum's photo
album. I used to think they were photos of me because the two of us
look the same save for my dad's ability to grow facial hair. Me, on the
other hand, I can only grow pathetic little patches here and there.

My kokum had two photos of my dad that are now mine. I
showed them to Tias.

In one of them, he's in the middle of the bush, smiling at the
camera. He's wearing these grey khaki shorts, and his legs are bare
and thin. His hands are pressed against his bare belly. There are gaps
between his upper teeth, making him look a little like Madonna. I
run my tongue along the same teeth in my mouth and feel the same
gaps. That's me, I think. Someone has superimposed my face onto the
body of some boy in the '60s. But his body has no baby fat whereas my
boy-body was plump. I guess those genetics jumped a generation too.

In the second photo, my dad is a teenager, and his hair is jet black
and shaggy, curly at the tips. Looking at the photo, you would swear
he was Latin, in fact, he looks exactly like Cheech Marin. He's sitting
in the hallway of what looks like his school, his long, lanky legs spread
wide apart, one extended and the other bent into an 'A.' There is a
German shepherd nuzzling its head against his shoulder. My dad's

arms are wrapped around the dog; he cradles it with such affection, you'd think it was his kid. I think the photo explains my childhood propensities for running around on all fours like a dog. Hell, maybe it even explains my love for doggy-style.

Tias was the first person I ever showed these photos to. He smiles and nods whenever I tell him what I think of my father. Talking of men pleases him. On one such occasion, I was in the tub, and he played with my hair through the whole ordeal. I was half asleep when he asked if I wanted to go shoot some hoops. I shook my head and sank deeper into the bath.

"You need to stop feeling so sorry for yourself," Tias said as he left the bathroom. I heard his distorted voice from beneath the surface. When I heard his footsteps pounding down the stairs, I blew bubbles in the water. I wanted to tell Tias that if I don't feel me—well, then no one ever would.

XXX

When I awoke, Tias was gone. The smell of fried bologna and burnt toast wafted into the room. I rolled over onto the other side of the bed. His pillow smelled of his sweat and musk. I pressed my face against it and imagined my cheeks brushing against his fine chest hairs. I got hard. My fingers had memorized the musculature of his body—I could feel the cool prick of his hard nipple against my forearm. When I licked the back of my teeth, I could taste his tongue.

It was when I raised my face from the pillow that I saw the photo. Tucked neatly into the corner of Tias's mirror was a photo of him kissing Jordan Blackhorse—the girl I'd come to love-hate. She was tall and beautiful, with long black hair and sultry, bedroom eyes. She was an intimidating soul wrapped up in a dainty frame; as cute as she looked, she was tough as nails—hell, one time she'd even given Logan a black eye when he called her a cheap slut. She was also blessed with the motherlode of all names. I abhorred her tenacity throughout school because of it; I always wondered if having a boy's name made for a boy's mind. That, and everyone knew she was NDN without having to ask. See, you know you're a legit Nate when your surname combines a colour with an animal. She used to say that her NDN name was Tatanka, and everyone was always impressed at her soliloquies spoken in her Saulteaux tongue. I later learned that Tatanka meant buffalo in Lakota. My kokum taught me that one night while we were watching wrestling.

"Blackhorse? That family is a bunch of looneys, m'boy," she said, rolling her eyes.

"I want to be like Jordan," I said. "I love her NDN name."

"And what is it? Great Black Angry Bear?" she roared over Steve Austin screaming on TV.

"Tatanka."

"Tatanka?" She laughed. "Tatanka? She's nothing but stories and lies, m'boy. That tongue of hers, it's a smoke screen—them Blackhorses, they're known for their tongues."

"What do you mean?"

"Well, for starters," she proudly announced, "the girl's Saulteaux and speaking Lakota. Tatanka means buffalo in Lakota. Rule number one, if you want to be an NDN, you might want to do your research first."

I giggled and flung my feet into the air. My kokum caught them with her hands and placed them on her lap. Her hands were wrinkled but firm as she pressed her thumbs squarely into the balls of my feet and squeezed upwards towards my toes. Press, pull, slide, and release. She used to do this to me when I was a baby and later as a young boy. She'd pull my breath and sadness and jealousy and rage from me and expunge it through my feet.

"The feet hold in them all sorts of mysteries," she said softly. "Our footprints, they carry with them all sorts of stories. You can burn my prints, cut my hair, salt my tongue, but these stories are etched into the hides of our soles. And yours," she continued, "yours are arched like a crescent, like a moon. You're not flatfooted like me. Heck, boy, your feet tell the story of opaskwuwipizun."

"The opa-what?"

"Your feet are the story of when ducks begin to molt—the full moon in July."

Jordan's picture was still staring at me in Tias's bed. Being watched like that, I felt ashamed in my nakedness. I covered my junk with Tias's blanket and stared up at the ceiling. I couldn't stop thinking of her and Tias holding each other, of how her body fit his more honestly than mine. I got up, got dressed, and pocketed the photo.

Upstairs, I could hear the sound of forks scraping against plates. Tias didn't invite me up to join him and his family for breakfast—he was hiding me in his basement bedroom like a rat. I wondered if Jordan had been here too. Had he invited her upstairs for breakfast? I knew he liked her. Did this mean they were snagging? Is this what he liked? I pulled the photo from my pocket and studied it. *I could be that,* I thought. *From here on out I'll charge an extra buck per hour.* My repertoire was growing with new roles I could perform. My mind was becoming a funhouse of femininity. I stuck the photo back onto Tias's mirror and headed toward the window to leave.

When he fucks me, I wondered, *does he think, "I wish my woman was here?" Or is it the other way around—when he fucks her, does he think of me?*

XXXI

Once I left the rez, I made a small circle of friends—some of them were once my clients or Grindr hook-ups, others were Nates who had left the rez too. Most of us were sad-looking kids wearing hand-me-downs and Sally Ann; we had a propensity for drinking too much and dancing too fiercely. I ended up becoming better friends with Jordan after she moved to Winnipeg, even if she was sleeping with Tias—I mean, we hung out once in a while on the rez because we had to, limited space, y'know? Even more limited when it came to sharing the same boy too, but us NDNs know a few things about trading resources. She was the baddest of the crew because she was a neechi from Bloodvein. All she had to say was that she was from Bloodvein and then no one would fuck with her. Everyone knew that Blood Nates were ferocious and that the women were tough as wolverines. She was one of those real traditional Nates who always scared me— the kind whose gait looked like a jingle dance and whose arms were thick as logs because her daddy taught her how to trap. Her mom died giving birth to her and Jordan used that story to scare people off. "I've killed someone before, y'know," she'd say while pushing up her sleeves. "What chance do you think a punk like you has?" She was scary as fuck and I took to her like a magnet knowing full well the protection she could offer. That was how I survived the rez, annit? Making friends with the toughest NDN women I could find because everyone knows that Nate girls are tougher than the men. Sometimes they'd fight at parties, the girls and the boys, and while the boys would sometimes win, the girls would attack like vicious packs of wolves and they never forgot a grudge. An eye for an eye was their motto. If you pissed them off, if you looked at them the wrong way, if you stole one of their men—they'd all remember and they'd come back at you when you were least expecting it. In this way, they had miraculous memories—hell, we all struggled to memorize BEDMAS and the periodic table, but boy let me tell you, if you ever crossed one of them, they'd remember it until they got their revenge. Better to fess up and take your beating, cuz it ain't healthy to live with that kind of fear residing in you.

Jordan and I only became real friends when she finally found out that I had been sexting her man—prior, I think she kind of knew, since she always kept an eye on me in the hallways and in the smoking pit. She gave me a damn good lickin, that's for sure, but afterwards, when she felt my debt had been paid, she helped me up and said, "So, you wanna get lunch, 'er what?" She took me down to the McDonald's on Portage. Portage was the street where all the Nates hung out, aside from the North End—you didn't have to worry about looking fancy or talking straight down there because everyone talked the same; so long as you weren't white, you could make it around pretty safely. Lots of Filipinos down there too, but we got along pretty well—we all fished for catfish in the Red and tried to look out for one another at house parties.

Inside McDonald's, she pulled out a giant book of coupons she was carrying around in her backpack. "Work smart," she said, "not hard." Half those coupons were old as shit but she knew where to take them, the right fast-food joints and grocery stores—places where she could either befriend or intimidate the other brown-skins. At the counter she marched right up to the cashier, this young Nate kid, slapped down her coupon, and said, "Two Big Macs and large fries, cuz—and don't forget, it's two-for-one." Her coupon had expired but the boy rang her through anyway—maybe out of respect, maybe out of fear. Fuck, she scared the shit out of me, but as we sat down she flashed me a goofy smile. "For fucksakes, boy, you can sure take a heck of a beating," she said, laughing, and handed me a wet wipe from her pocket to clean up the blood and snot that had apparently dried around my nostrils.

As we talked, Jordan would continue to burst into fits of laughter, stopping only long enough to punch me in the arm. She always did that—make her laugh, you got a beating; piss her off, you got a beating, there was no walking away without a bruise from her.

With her, I was convinced that having a boy's name could certainly make for a boy's mind.

XXXII

Tias stood behind me and his brown hands were around mine, our fingers interlaced like a woven basket. We held our cigarettes in this way, then flicked the wheel on our lighter, waiting for the spark to catch. Schht, schht, schht—we struck the lighter's stone for what seemed like minutes, trying to will the flame to burst through. Schht, schht, schht.

"Ah, fuck this," Tias said. "I'll just go start the goddamn element, do it the old-fashioned way, eh?"

We decided to try and quit smoking cold turkey after a few weeks of me hacking up phlegm all night. "It's white," he said, scooping up the spittle from my chin. "That's good, your body is tryna clean you out." We thought it was a good idea to quit smoking for a while, since, well, we didn't have a lot of money between us, and besides, we could bum enough off the kids at parties if we needed. No use buying cigarettes when you can get them for free from your cousins, eh? But while that idea sounded good in theory, it quickly backfired on us. After only one day, we decided we couldn't do it. We came to the understanding that quitting cold turkey wasn't going to work for us; it had to be slow, easy, one day at a time. So on our second day we agreed to allow ourselves one cigarette, and only in the mornings. After we had our single smoke, we saved two for the following day, then cut up the rest and threw them into the garbage. But when I went to take my shower and realized I forgot my towel, I came out of the bathroom and found Tias fashioning a broken cigarette back together using the tape from a lint roller.

"Okay, so two a day then?" I said.

We stuck to two that day and chewed a lot of gum instead. We felt proud of ourselves. Tias, unable to stay the night, asked if I'd walk him home so I could make sure he didn't bum or buy any cigarettes. I agreed and saw him as far as the Marlborough where he hopped on a bus. He waved goodbye and I smiled at him. It was getting dark and the wind was cold and my nipples were sticking up through my shirt. By now I'd usually light a cigarette to warm my bones and count how many I'd need to get back home, usually one every block or two. I began walking back to my apartment, but the urge crept up my body, from my kneecaps to my fingers, which were aching to curl around a filter, like the delicate digits of Audrey Hepburn.

I turned around and told myself, *Just one*, then made my way to O'Calcutta. I bought a pack of Pall Malls for ten bucks, took one out, and lit it up. That feeling of relaxation came over me, the kind that burns your throat but makes you feel like you're back home even if you're hundreds of miles away. A good cigarette is like a familiar story. A Nate saw me spark one up and made his way over to me.

"Hey cuz, can I bum a light?"

"Oh yeah, sure."

"Oh hey, can I bum a smoke too?"

Damn trickster, I thought, *someone's taught him well.* I laughed, handed him a few, and then continued on my way home. I told myself to throw out the pack because Tias and I had made a promise to one another. *I will when I'm at home. Yeah right, do it now. Okay, okay.* So I tossed them aside, disgusted at myself for wasting ten dollars on a single cigarette and handing them out like Popeye's candies to randoms. What was I, made of money? My mom would have given me a good lickin if she found out I had not only wasted cigarettes but money too. I made it about twenty steps before I turned around to fish them back out from the bin and put them back in my pocket. *Can still use them even if I don't smoke them*, I thought. *Always good for ceremony.*

I stood there on my balcony, cigarette in my fingers, and the lighter flicking hard against its stone. Schht, schht, schht—my eyes began to lose the ability to focus, the bright flares of the lighter imprinted into my retinas. When I closed my eyes, I saw those squiggles of light on the back of my lids. Lights jagged, sharp like lightning, and bursting into a million little dots that lit up what looked like a city. I opened my eyes again, they were watering now, the edge of the flint still being dragged through metal. It was a soft groove by now and my thumb was sore from flicking the lighter.

I looked down but only saw light, light like an egg·blanketed in darkness, my vision was a circle, and there, in the middle of it all, was the red glow of Tias's cigarette burning like a comet. *This,* I told myself, *must be how worlds are made.*

"Tee, you coming up, 'er what?" I said. "Element's redder than the devil's dick."

"Well?" he said, exhaling. "You gonna stand up there and stare at me for an hour like I'm some wannabe Wilson?"

He was trying his damnedest to stump me on a Tom Hanks joke

ever since last week. We had been watching *Captain Phillips* and I convinced him it was the prequel to *Cast Away*. He believed me and tried to lecture Jordan on the intricacies of Hank's filmic history, turns out she gave him a slap upside the head. "Idiot," she said, "you just told me that *Cast Away* is about some guy named Chuck Noland and then you go and try and tell me that *Captain Phillips* is him before he crashes? How in the hell that make sense?" He later bitched me out for tricking him like that.

"Tick-tock, doc, you gonna stand there like a stick in the mud all damn night?" he said when I didn't respond.

"Coming," I said, my eyesight returning to normal. Funny, that boy might not know his movies, but he knew a thing or two about hustling time. Tick-tock, eh? Made sense if we live and die by the clock.

XXXIII

There are only a few sounds that always hurt me and one of them is the sound of my mom crying. It seems like my mom is always in tears on the phone with someone who is either dying or in pain, or knows someone who is. There aren't enough jokes in the world to stop her from weeping and there aren't enough stories to stop me from feeling. I think that's why she turns to the bottle and why I sometimes follow. But regardless of her bouts of drinking, I love being around my mom. Like with my kokum, I used to like to watch her put on her makeup for the night, although sometimes I thought Momma's bordered more on drag than natural, which made me love the process all the more. She had a knack for experimentation when it came to getting into full-face with only drugstore makeup and a lip pencil shaved down to a nub. My mom took a great deal of pride in her makeup routines. One night she meticulously explained her process to me.

"This colour right here? This is eyeshadow, but you can also use it to colour your lips if you're out of lipstick, remember that. And if you're out of liner, you can always use your lipstick."

I nodded vigorously, diligently noting her tips.

"You want to snag yourself a man? Then you best slather this shit around your eyes, really smoke them out. You want to be like smoke yourself, you know? These boys smudge for good luck to snag on the pow wow trail, well, m'boy, what you want to do is beat them at their own game. Smoke your eyes and they'll be begging to smudge you. That's a fact."

I noted this too.

"And if you really want to make sure you win them over, there are only two accessories you need: a damn good perfume and a hell of a lot of confidence. Even if you have to fake the latter. And heck, you can fake smelling good too. Take some ashes from Kokum's smudging bowl and rub it into the hollows of your jaw. You'll snag yourself a mighty fine piece, m'boy. A mighty fine piece, just like your momma did."

Now instead of putting on makeup she cries on the phone, her eyes puffy and her lips constantly cracked. I don't tell her that sometimes when I'm on the phone, I hang up and I cry too—all those tears collecting into a pool on my desk. I used to wonder if I might run out of tears; that if I kept crying, all that saltwater would conjure up a whole new ocean. Sometimes I imagined that when I shook my hair, Sky Woman fell out of it; she'd look up at me and say, "Baby, you're home," and I'd say, "Momma, this for you too."

XXXIV

The year that I came out to the people back on the rez, I had this one cousin who texted me that if he ever saw me, he'd kick the living shit out of me. As much as I wanted to go home then, I sure as hell didn't want to make that a reality. When I told Jordan this, she said she'd come back to the rez with me: "I'll fix his wagon," she said, a phrase she stole from her dad after her baby was taken away a few years back. She threw a house party one night after her daughter had gone to sleep, but it turns out she did mushrooms and went on a hardcore trip. Family services stepped in the next day and labelled her an unfit mother. "She was my rainbow baby," she says when she's drunk. "Supposed to make everything better. My aunties told me that a baby fixes things." I never met her daughter, but knew that her kid was her life—her entire fridge was plastered with pics of her. "Madilyn took after her momma," she said once. "Piss her off and she'd get mad as a goddamn coyote." I always wondered just what in the hell fixing a wagon had to do with giving someone a beat-down, but these were the types of questions you never asked Jordan.

"Treat him like a buffalo," she also said as she cracked her knuckles, referring to my cousin. "Smash his ol' head in."

I never took her up on that offer, I didn't want to go there and end up with a bloodied face—hell, I wasn't the one from Bloodvein. So we partied at her house instead. She called up her friends, who were all pretty cool, and told them to come on down, but only if they had chip-ins. We all scrambled enough cash to get a two-four and some whisky from Peggy, who horded alcohol like gold—she was smart that way, stealing bottles and selling them during holidays, or pow wows, or reserving them for after-parties where she'd sell them for twice their worth. Desperate times called for desperate measures as they say, annit? The whisky, though, was a poor choice on our end because everyone knows whisky does two things to us: makes us rowdy, or nostalgic as all hell. But we gathered up a good crew of people—most of them Nate, but she knew a couple East Indian guys who did stick-and-poke tattoos and sold them to rich white kids who thought they were traditional henna. All us NDNs, I thought, sure know how to turn pennies into bills.

We had a little gathering at her place, a room full of brownness in a shoddy apartment down on Magnus Avenue. We could be as loud as we wanted to be—Jordan's neighbours knew not to file any noise complaints on account of how her screams of rage could shake their walls and knock down portraits. We played that drinking game "Never Have I Ever" which was pretty slack because it was super easy to get me out, all they had to do was say "never have I ever sucked a dick" and I would immediately lose. As we grew drunker, we slapped on A Tribe Called Red and had our own stadium pow wow. None of us knew the words but we sang along anyways, "way, yah, hey-ya-how." We thought we were hardcore traditionalists, but we probably sounded like a pack of rez dogs. We did shots of whisky, danced to electronic pow wow, and hugged each other and cried all night. That's how NDNs are, once the firewater kicks in we all become straight-up storytellers. We said prayers for dead cousins, for the stillborn, for the friends we lost in snowmobile accidents. Hell, we cried for those we didn't even know—so-and-so's cousin who we met once who died from fentanyl, or that girl who OD'd in the band office last year. That's how NDNs become friends, though, over a good story, a damn good cry, and then a right righteous laugh when the next little NDN pulls up in a rezzed-out van. "Holy hell," we'd all say in unison, "look at Fred Flintstone over here." That night we drank into the wee hours of the morning and one of Jordan's friends got drunk enough to think that his reflection in the mirror was his dancing partner; he punched his own reflection and tore his knuckle up pretty good. "Howa, he's just snapped," someone said, which made Jordan laugh. "Oh heck, that guy's feeling no pain," she said. That saying is weird, "feeling no pain." I used to laugh at it too, but nowadays I think that they're drunk because they're feeling all kinds of pain.

In that tiny living room with lawn chairs for furniture and an air mattress in the corner, we all danced until our feet were blistered. We linked arms in a circle, feeling the music we loved but in a language that haunted us. And of course, little ol' gay me vogued in the middle of the circle—a little Willi Ninja went a long way to a bunch of breeders, but you know, you got to earn your street cred somehow. They round danced around me at a pace that seemed impossible, until the room was spinning, the lights weaving in between their bodies, and me, sweaty, crusty-eyed, and horny as all hell, slowly lounging into a half-baked death drop while they cheered, thinking I was some goddamn ballet dancer.

"This ceremonial enough for ya, Jon?" Jordan shouted.

"Hah, not even—" I jested.

But truth be told, I wanted that—me, time-stepping in the middle of a group of Nates, dancing like Kokum taught me whenever the "Red River Jig" came on NCI radio.

XXXV

Tias and Jordan drove in from the rez and helped me move to a new apartment from the North End to the Exchange—the rent there had a decline after they called it Canada's "most racist city" and that lawyer's wife went on an NDN rant. It was always a little weird when the three of us were together. They both gave me housewarming gifts: Jordan brought her smudging bowl and a coil of sweet grass for the house, while Tias got me a crock pot he picked up at a garage sale. Inside I found a pressed daisy and a little note, "Dinner soon?" Tias winked at me as he watched me take out the flower. Jordan wasn't stupid, she knew what was going on between us but turned a blind eye because of how long we had been friends. She never asked about it in the same way that I never asked about them.

After we were done, Jordan told us to put on our jigging shoes because she was ready to dance. I called up ol' Peggy and had her sell us a bottle from her stash; she gave me a discount like usual because she had been so close with my kokum. She delivered us a two-six of El Dorado rum and charged us thirty bones plus a chip-in for gas. She always delivered her goods in person—brought cigarettes to the moms who couldn't make it out of the house, Percs to the kids who were "feeling no pain," McDonald's to the crews of Nates hungover as all hell. We asked her if she wanted to come in for a drink—she was one of those dealers who had no qualms about dipping into her own cache.

"So-where-you-kids-headed-eh?" she said. She always spoke like she was in a hurry, rarely taking breaths between words. It always confused anyone who wasn't from the rez.

"Ask Jonny, it's his day," Jordan said.

"I'm thinking—maybe, Fame?"

"Oh-that's-the-ol'-gay-bar-eh?"

"Yeah," I said, a little embarrassed. I still always felt a wave a shame rush through my body whenever someone might associate me with being Two-Spirit, even if Tias and Jordan were bordering there too.

"I-heard-they-play-the-best-music," Peggy said with a giggle, then playfully slapped Jordan on the arm, who shaded her with a side-eye before laughing and slapping her back. Peggy had a great sense of humour. A lot of people didn't like her because they thought she overcharged them on her sales, but she had to make a living too, annit? She told us a story of how she once threw her back out while working at a Burger King—she slipped on a bun that had fallen on the floor, ruptured a disc in her back. She ended up getting a prescription for Percocets with Dr Levi, the doctor downtown. All the Nates went to him because he had used to work on the northern reserves. Maybe he got more money for working with the Nates, but he had a roster of them as patients, in fact there were so many coming in with all different kinds of pain that he usually only had a few minutes to spend with each of them. And you know us NDNs, we're good storytellers, you could earn a living that way if you wanted. Peggy did, playing up her chronic pains, and getting a monthly prescription for Percs, which she sold for $10 a pop, $12 if she had to deliver them. So a monthly scrip could earn close to a grand, which paid for her rent and left her with enough cash to send to her kid. She thought she was doing a good thing, selling clean Percs to people who needed them, saving them from a fentanyl overdose, but we all knew she was enabling others— hell, sometimes you have to do what you have to do to survive.

"Oh yeah, you wanna come?" I said.

"Maybe-yeah-I'll-have-to-see-okay-gotta-few-deliveries-to-make-yet."

Peggy may not have been everyone's fave person, but I had mad respect for a woman who could make ends meet for herself. Sometimes survival can be a hell of a game—we all knew when we moved off the rez, but living in the city was a whole different animal. Who was I to judge? We gave her a hearty cheer and hug.

"Okay-call-me-if-you-need-a-ride-later-okay?"

She had this way about her, a motherly instinct that she extended to everyone she knew. Sure, she'd charge you an arm and a leg to bring you a bottle, but if you knew someone who OD'd or needed a ride to rehab, she had your back—free of charge. We all needed Peggy, even if we rarely said so.

"Will do, Peg, drive safe," I said.

"Okay-yeah-okay-love-you-bye," she said, and then soon after we heard her car take off like a bat out of hell back down Princess. I loved how she always punctuated her sentences with "okay" like a true-blue rez girl, and how she told you she loved you every time she said goodbye. The last time I talked to my kokum while drunk, I told her I loved her—but it killed me that I had to be drunk to do it.

"Man, that woman has the energy of three men," Tias said. We made some fresh drinks with the rum Peg delivered and then Tias and Jordan sat on the couch cuddled up against one another while I sat on a lawn chair across from them.

I caught Tias stealing a glance at me every now and then, but I ignored it while Jordan was right there beside him. We decided to play a game of Fuck the Dealer and downed drinks much faster than we anticipated, but that's the thing with us NDNs, we're competitive as all hell and hate losing.

"Jordan, drink two," I said.

"Oh, you just made a powerful enemy, my friend."

She laughed, then punched Tias in the arm. I was happy it wasn't me being hit this time. I could hate her, I tried to, but she had a fucking redeeming quality about her that reminded me of my kokum— they were both little women with the ferocious power of a behemoth inside them. Jordan said she wanted to put some makeup on, so I let her borrow my collection. She decided on applying a thick-ass Cara Delevigne brow—they say your brows don't need to be sisters but at least cousins, well, hers were cousins who hooked up on the pow wow trail and found out they were related in the morning. While she was still in the bathroom, Tias patted the seat beside him and motioned for me to sit with him. When I did, he pecked me on the cheek.

"What are you going to wear tonight?" he asked.

"You?" I joked, and then I kissed my fingers and slid them between his lips. "Probably just a shawl and a tee. You?"

"What you see is what you get."

"And what I see is what I want."

"Hey Jon, where's your mascara?" Jordan yelled from the bath-room.

"In the travel bag, the pink case."

"Better-Than-Sex?"

"Yeah. Benefit makes a solid mascara, waterproof too!"

"Cool, brah." She started humming a song that echoed off the bathroom tiles.

I went to my bedroom to change and Tias followed, asking if I had a shirt he could wear.

"You killing it and me looking like some homeless Nate. Hola, yeah right," he said.

He watched me as I slid my pants off and then my shirt. My rib-cage was poking through my chest and I felt pleased that my bones presented themselves to Tias.

"Can I borrow this lip liner?" Jordan yelled, rapping to Biggie now.

"You sure lost a lot of weight, Jon," Tias said.

"Not enough," I replied, feeling his eyes surveying my body.

He stood behind me, wrapped his arms around my waist, and pushed his pelvis against me with a hardness that could crack rocks. Ignoring him, I walked over to my closet, picked out a red plaid shirt, and threw it at him.

"Wear this, you'll look hella good in it," I said.

It had zippers up the sides so that you could be both classy and a little slutty. He took off his shirt and I eyed up the divot in the middle of his sternum, the sprouts of hair on his nipples. I wanted to touch him right then, to taste his musk, lick his pits—but I controlled myself, I wasn't a homewrecker. He buttoned up the plaid, tousled his hair, flashed me a smile. I laughed—the confidence on this boy—and zipped up the sides of his shirt; I took pride in being the first one of the night to touch him, feel the outline of his waist. He was a man built simply—and the sight of him gave me a hard-on.

"You owe me a dance tonight," I said, and winked. I wanted to taste him again, to swallow him like I owned him, for him to call me sexy and for me to believe it. I wanted him so fucking bad, I wanted him to say, "Me, too."

"Say it," I said.

He looked confused. "What?"

"Say it," I repeated.

"He looked sheepish.

"Just fucking say it, you pussy."

"Okay, okay. I love her, all right?"

It wasn't the response I was expecting. But before I could say anything, Jordan came out of the bathroom, her lids winged, her eyes the colour of rust, and her lips lined into some serious DSLs. But she wasn't wearing blush, and the foundation framed her face with a cakey pigment.

"Come here, Jord," I said, "let me add a little flair." Part of me wanted to say *me too*, part of me wanted to say *fuck you*.

I took her back into the bathroom, took out my Nars blush and fan brush, and applied a soft pink to her cheeks, then fanned it up towards her temples ever so slightly, giving her a beautiful sheen. She gasped when she saw herself in the mirror, and I thought at that moment that damn, I give good blush.

It was nine-thirty in the evening and we were all ready to jig our little hearts out. We each took a final shot, then called Peggy back for a ride to Fame. It was a hell of a lot cheaper than Duffy's or Unicity and we felt better knowing the money went to her. Once we arrived at the club, we learned it was men's night, so Tias and I got in for free, though Jordan intimidated the bouncer enough with her scowl for him to say, "Okay, yeah, you too." The bar crowd was more breeder than queer that night; when a couple of men came up to Jordan and asked to buy her a round, she took their drinks and told them, "Cheers, now fuck off." No one bought Jordan, you had to earn her—don't ask me how Tias did it. When she went outside for a smoke break, Tias bought me a shot of Fireball. As we waited for her to return, we stood at the bar and danced to Britney Spears' "Work Bitch." As the beats grew more intense, and Brit asked if we wanted a Maserati, Tias started grinding his hips against mine, and before I knew it our arms were wrapped around each other's waists and our chests were touching. A boy walked by and said, "You two are cute together," which made us laugh.

Tias pulled me even closer and whispered, "Don't ever change, man, you hear me? Don't ever change."

I'll always remember what he said, it stays in my head like it's another personal mantra. Tias and I separated our bodies a few moments before Jordan returned and then we all danced to Gloria

Gaynor, Missy Elliott, and Lady Gaga. Jordan pulled Tias in close and they began grinding to every song, including the slow ones. When I started feeling jealous, I went to the bar and let boys buy me drinks until I forgot all about it. I learned this trick on how to get drunks to buy you rounds. Tias and I bought these fake wedding rings from Wal-Mart and would wear them to bars and parties. When we told people we were recently engaged but couldn't afford a proper wedding, people would swoon and feel sorry for us—then they'd buy us a drink or sometimes two, and all you had to do was avoid them for the rest of the night. It was an easy way to go to a party with ten dollars and leave fucked up as shit. I pulled that card three times that night, those white suburban gays lived for that sentimental bull and bought me drinks like my life depended on it.

I got drunk pretty quickly, three shots in a row will do that to you—meanwhile, Tias and Jordan were still grinding on the dance floor and my petty levels started to go through the roof. I took one of the boys who bought me a drink by the hand and dragged him to the dance floor. We swayed to Rihanna's "We Found Love," our bodies pressed together like leather straps to a bundle of sage. He kissed my neck as I slid my hands down the back of his jeans—and I made sure that Tias saw us. He looked distraught, which turned me on, but then I saw Jordan whisper something to him, pointing at me. But I didn't care. I was on fire. I turned to watch the go-go boys with their twenty-eight-inch waists earn their fives and tens in their Andrew Christian underwear, their chests bare like skinned rabbits, their skin red from all the slaps and dirty money, then made dance-floor love with other boys who thought romance was a two-for-six shot of whisky and a dry hump on the stage. "Buckle up, ima give it to you stronger." We climbed onto the stage, but the bouncer said we had to take off our shirts to dance there and then he tried to remove mine. Eventually I had a smoke outside with a hobo named Mikhail who smoked from a pipe and every time he inhaled, he said the world was turning to ashes.

I came to in St. Boniface, on the steps of an apartment building, my jacket curled around my body. A couple walked past me speaking French: "Est ce que tu vas bien?" The only word I had to reply was "Têyi," but they thought I was speaking gibberish and threw me a toonie. A car drove by with the license plate "S3T H0M" and I thought, *Yeah, me too.* I sat on French steps not speaking a lick of French aside from Lil Kim's ruminations and knew that two a.m. had come much too quickly. I put my head in my hands and closed my eyes—then all of a sudden I felt a man grab me, his hands a revenant to my body's memory; he picked me up and threw me over his shoulders. I remember the lights of bursting cherries, the smell of rubbing alcohol, the sound of someone saying, "Yeah, I picked up another one."

I woke up in my own bed the next morning. I fashioned a cigarette out of butts left by Peggy and checked my phone. There was a text from Tias: "Text me when you wake up you fucking boozer!"

I fucked up, I knew that—but a part of me said: It's-okay-it's-okay-it's-okay, you're on your way now.

XXXVI

If you asked me what my kokum tasted like, I would tell you Bee Hive corn syrup. She put that thick golden syrup on everything: on our French toast, in her tea, drizzled over her jello cake. And she found every excuse in the book to use that syrup in other ways: to wash her hair, clean her face, and once, when I burned my hand on an element, she soothed my burn with it. Heck, she even kept a baby jar full of corn syrup in her first aid kit. "For 'mergencies," she'd always say. "You never know when someone's gonna fall into a shock."

One day when one of my aunties' blood sugar fell too low and she fainted, my kokum scooped her off the floor, cradled her neck in the crook of her elbow, and fed her a tablespoon of corn syrup. "It's magic," my kokum said. "This here is some magic in a two-dollar can." Sure enough, within thirty seconds my aunt roused back to life.

My kokum always stood by that magic, even as her diabetes began to consume her feet and legs. One of her kitchen shelves was completely lined with those bright yellow bottles. Nowadays, my mom makes fun of that shelf when we look at photos. "She loved that syrup so damn much that she even styled her hair after the goddamned bottle!" And in fact, it was true, my kokum's hair used to be coned into a beehive. While I may never understand my kokum's odd hairstyle choices, I will confess: I too can't stop myself from buying that syrup. Every time I'm sick, I still take a spoonful—and when my taste buds fizz with that familiar sweetness, it feels like I'm with Kokum again in her too warm home.

After she died, I found her recipe book tucked away in a box. It was the only keepsake of Kokum's I took: a little wooden box with a flower painted on the top. There were hundreds of recipes inside, all handwritten on an assortment of paper: napkins, cards, envelopes. There I found her famous recipe for sweet and sour meatballs, which everyone loved. I found myself staring at it and tracing my fingers along the fine ridges of her writing—she was the only person I knew who always wrote in cursive. I could see her whole life wrapped up inside that little box of wonders—the loops of her "l's" and "t's" are perfect in the recipes she wrote when she was young, but her later entries are increasingly harder to read, as her hands became hardened by arthritis.

One day on a whim, I decided to make her meatballs. Kokum usually used ground-up elk or deer meat, but all I had was some regular hamburger. I cracked an egg, crushed up some saltine crackers, diced a week-old onion, and kneaded it all together. I tried to be meticulous, like Kokum taught me to be—patience makes for a delicious dinner. I folded the meat mixture into itself, then rolled it into fat little balls, trying to keep them as uniform as possible, and then I fried them up in a pan, giving each one the love it deserved. I layered them gently in my crock pot, sprinkled salt and pepper over them, and closed the lid.

The sauce was the hardest part: two cups of ketchup, brown sugar, vinegar, and soy sauce, in a pot over high heat. But you have to keep stirring. I used to watch my kokum at the stove stirring her pot, the wobble of the loose skin beneath her arms—skin we used to call her bingo wings—but also the flexing of her hard muscles as she stirred.

"I learned this from the Hutterites, m'boy," she said once as I watched. "The Waldners, they're nice folk."

When I was a kid, one of the trailers on the rez caught fire and killed two young boys. Later, everyone on the rez had a feast in their honour. The Waldners, a white family who lived across the fields, arrived to pay their respects in a procession of large white vans. They took off their hats, placed them on their chests, and shook the elders' hands, who greeted them with toothless smiles. The Waldner women came bearing trays of food: chicken, pies, perogies, and those sweet and sour meatballs. Boy, everyone ate good that night. After dinner, the family of the deceased spoke about their boys and how they were learning to become firekeepers, about how they died when one of them passed out with a lit cigarette. The Waldners then told us about how they had lost a boy recently too in a farming accident. My kokum spent the evening talking with the Waldner women, sharing sewing tips and recipes, including the one for the meatballs—she wrote it down right there on a napkin.

When my sauce started to come together, I thickened it with cornstarch and water. Still, it was runnier than my kokum's, and tasted more sweet than sour, but it would do. I poured the sauce atop the meatballs in the slow cooker, tossed everything together, and let it simmer for a few hours. When it was nearly done, I texted Tias: "Dinner tonight?" and it took only a few minutes before I could hear footsteps barreling down the hallway.

"Heck those smell right good," Tias said, opening the lid.

"Get outta there, for godsakes," I said, slapping his hand away.

"Just a little sample, make sure you did it right."

I rolled my eyes. "Go ahead then." Tias never had no patience, that boy. I stuck a teaspoon into the bubbling sauce and gave it to him. He slurped it down, but it burned his mouth, which made him stick out his tongue and pant like a dog—like I said, no patience whatsoever.

"Let it simmer for a bit yet," I said.

"Whatchu wanna do while we wait?"

We decided to cab it to Wal-Mart, which was every urban NDN's favourite pastime. We scanned the aisles and looked at the furniture, fantasizing about what kind of houses we'd have when we really grew up and had money.

"What do you wanna have with the meatballs?" Tias asked.

"Hell, I used up about every bit of food I had to make those."

Tias took out his wallet, emptied his coat and jeans pockets, and pooled together a few dollars in change. "Prolly got enough here for a box of Stovetop, maybe two." He had an obsession with that stuffing and it was about the only food he could cook well besides those old Cheemo perogies. So we bought a couple boxes and cabbed back to my place. Tias's mom had an account with the cab companies that she said was for emergencies, but we figured having a side dish to go with our dinner was excuse enough—so we charged our bill to her account.

Tias made his stuffing and took pride in his work as he fluffed it up with a fork. We then gorged ourselves on our meal, which basically was hamburger and wet croutons—but it hit the spot. Afterwards on my couch, I spooned him from behind and we watched a movie on his cellphone, thanks to my neighbour's wifi. I stroked his head and felt the spot where his hair was missing.

"You never did tell me what happened here," I said.

"Ah, it's nothing."

I braided my leg through his and nibbled on his shoulder. "C'mon, don't be slack."

He turned around to face me. "I don't know, it's stupid."

"Tell me," I said.

"So I guess I used to have long hair as a kid, you know? My mom liked it a lot, said it looked handsome, but my dad said I looked like a queer." He shuffled closer to me, put his hand on the patch of skin. "You remember when we had to do that fundraising for the Fishermen? Selling chocolates and shit? Don't know why the fuck we were selling chocolates when just about every house on the rez had a kid in school—shoulda just had an ol' booze bingo, y'know?"

We had two methods of fundraising on the rez: we'd either throw a big social, invite the community, get everyone drunk off four-dollar drinks, and then hope we raked in enough, or else we'd have a booze bingo. The booze bingo always attracted lots of people, especially the elders, who played twenty cards at once like goddamn automatons and still had time to check other people's cards around them—"Oh, you missed B12, dear"; and of course the adults who brought their kids to help boost their chances. Everyone wanted a chance to win a bottle, especially the Texas mickey, either for themselves or to sell it and triple the money they spent. And when you did win, everyone knew about it and sucked up to you hardcore until it was gone.

Back then was when you'd catch ol' Peggy front and centre,

throwing down twenties for cards, arranging her good-luck charms in front of her. "Okay-am-I-winning-someone-check!" she'd yell at her neighbours, trying desperately to keep up with the calls. It took a special kind of NDN to want to sit beside her during bingo. She always had her eyes on that Texas mickey, and got mad every time she lost it, which was a lot.

"Yeah, I remember," I said to Tias.

"So I sold some boxes down at the gas station, mostly to white folks driving through. I told them if they bought a couple boxes I'd let them use my treaty number so they could save the tax on a fill-up. And this old woman bought three, but I guess she gypped me without me noticing, gave me a fiver instead of a ten. So I go home, right? And my dad counts my money, checks my stashes, tells me I'm missing some cash."

Those chocolate fundraisers were discontinued after two years because we used the cash like a personal bank. My mom would take the money I earned, leave an "IOU thirty" note in the envelope, and go buy groceries and smokes. It was always so goddamned embarrassing returning the envelope to your teacher and telling them sorry, your mom needed the cash.

"So he grabs me by the collar of my coat, pushes me up against the wall, lifts me off the floor. He says, 'Oh fer fuck sakes, you're useless, you know that? You go get that goddamn money right now!' and left me dangling there in the air, feet stretching to the floor, my cheeks turning red because my coat was pressing into my throat."

And we never could pay back those IOUs, so the money would

be owing on my account. "Jonny owes thirty dollars" hung over my head like I was a goddamn Sims avatar. I couldn't take out library books, couldn't go on the school computers, couldn't sign out gym equipment.

"And I tell him, 'Chill, man, it's just five dollars' and then he lets go of me and I slump to the floor, y'know? And that sets him off. 'Just five dollars?' he says, 'You don't know nothing of responsibility, boy, just five dollars, why I oughta take five dollars outta your ass right now.' And he takes off his belt and I know that that man could brand your ass like a steer, so I take off, right?"

When I visited my kokum, she asked, "C'mere m'boy what's wrong?" and I told her I was too embarrassed to go to school any-more—that the kids knew about my IOUs, and they made fun of my clothes, which all came from the Sally Ann. My kokum dug out her purse from beneath her chair, wrote me a cheque, gave me a kiss on the forehead, and told me not to tell my mother.

"But as I'm running away he grabs me by my coat—why the fuck did I used to wear that big-ass coat anyways? Always got me in trou-ble. And I squirm my way out of it so I can get away and then he grabs a chunk of my hair and yanks me back, pulls the hair clean out."

My kokum was as poor as they came, she only lived off a small bit of CPP and welfare cheques that was barely enough to pay for her medicine.

"And then I'm squirming on the floor, my hair still in his hands, him horrified for a second, my head bleeding. 'Ah, it's about time you got a man's haircut anyways' he says to me, 'get rid of that mop of a head you call hair." And he sits me down at the kitchen table, pulls a metal bowl out from the cupboard, grabs a pair of kitchen shears, gives my hair a bowl cut so I look like a fucking Beatle."

"You should have called me," I said. "I would have given you a stellar weave."

Tias laughs, then we are both quiet. We start watching the movie on his phone again.

I press my lips against the back of his head, feel his bald spot, which makes him wince. I curl myself around him tighter.

XXXVII

When I was thirteen we had something called Culturama at school. Everyone was divided into groups and assigned a country, and then learned about its terrain, its population, and its foods. Ours was Sweden. I was with three keeners, all of them white. Brooke, a blonde-haired girl who liked to wear glittery silver headbands, took charge of our group, claiming she was an expert on Sweden because her room was outfitted with IKEA furniture. She used IKEA-speak with words like "Malm" and "Hemnes," and described her colour schemes such as "bone white" and "mahogany brown." She looked me dead in the eye when she said the word "brown." I took some pride in the discomfort it caused her.

We each had to prepare a Swedish dish. "I'll make Swedish meatballs," Brooke announced. "I've had authentic ones before, you know, when my mom took me to IKEA."

Brooke then decided who would make what.

"Carol, you'll make gingersnap cookies. Tammy, can you do crêpes? And—"

Before she could finish, I interrupted her. "I can make rice pudding, my mom makes it all the time!"

It was true—my mom did make the best rice pudding. She'd make it for me as a reward whenever I came home with good news, like the time I had won our monthly spelling bee competition. I used to practise in my room at night to learn how to spell. I flicked my tongue at the harsh "T" in trade and puckered my lips into a kiss to lull out the "O" in goat.

There were all kinds of strange words that I knew how to spell then, like P-e-r-c-o-c-e-t and i-n-s-u-l-i-n.

My mom made her rice pudding with wild rice and smoothed it out with fresh milk. Then she added vanilla and cinnamon to it, which made it soft brown in colour. Raisins were next, and I liked to watch them fatten up in the froth of milk and cinnamon.

I also liked to help with the stirring. "Constant movement," she used to tell me, "helps to blend all of the flavours together and thicken the liquid. If you keep the rice and the raisins moving, they'll really fill up with milk." So I kept on stirring that pot. Which was hard; my biceps weren't half the size of my mom's—heck, mine were more the thickness of a hind's feet.

Whenever I complained that my arms were getting sore, my mom would take over. "Boy, you're slack," she'd say, and playfully slug me on the shoulder. To celebrate the day I finished high school, she made an entire soup pot full of rice pudding. As she stirred it with one arm, she pulled me in close with the other. She held me like that for what seemed like forever. I could feel her deep breaths on my hair, which sounded almost animal-like, but her touch was soft, and she rubbed the top of my head with her chin.

"Heck, I'm just proud of you m'boy," she said.

"Thanks Mom," I said. She didn't say that very often.

That night, all of our neighbours and family came to visit. My mom had cooked enough rice pudding for the entire rez. She ladled out bowl after bowl of pudding for the elders and kids who lined up first, and then again for everyone else. Some of my aunties brought bannock, and another had hamburger soup. My uncles brought moose meat burgers and grilled them up, and my kokum served her jello cake. Almost everyone I knew had come and were dressed up to some degree, which meant blue jeans instead of sweatpants. Someone brought a fiddle and played music. My mom and Roger danced on the grass outside, and my kokum swayed along with my younger cousins. We ate our feast and held each other into the wee hours of the night, until we couldn't see each other in the thickness of the dark.

Brooke had insisted that I bring Swedish rice pudding to Culturama, but when I showed up with mom's version instead, she gasped and shook her head. "Nonononono," she said. "This isn't Swedish rice pudding—why are there raisins in this? Why is it all brown? No, Jonny, you messed this up. We're all going to get an F because of you!"

I came home crying that night. "That's just the way it is," my mom said as she consoled me. That was the only answer she had whenever there was a problem. When I showed her the folder containing all the research we had done, she was really impressed. "Heck, they eat reindeer? Maybe we have more in common than I thought," she said. When she flipped to the last page, which was about the Swedish tradition of blood pudding, she started laughing, which echoed throughout our house. "Here, m'boy, I have just the thing," she said, and got up.

She pulled out all the frozen cherries she had in the freezer, and every packet of red Kool-Aid she could find, then threw them all into a pot along with some homemade raspberry jam and ketchup. When it came to a boil, she mushed the mixture until it was smooth and poured it all into a big plastic bowl.

"Here, you take this tomorrow instead," she said.

"The heck is this?"

"You tell them that if it's tradition they want, then this here is as close as it gets."

When I brought it to class the next day, everyone in our group gasped. "Here," I said to Brooke, "it's blood pudding, like the one we wrote about." I scooped a spoonful of the thick, maroon-coloured paste and held it near her lips. "Try it," I said, "it's a delicacy in Sweden." When she put the spoon into her mouth, she promptly spit it out all over our table. The map of Sweden that we had coloured was stained with cherries and ketchup.

"This tastes like *shit!*" she screamed. Our teacher immediately stormed over and handed us both pink slips to see the principal. Brooke's tongue and lips were stained red; I laughed as she pawed at her mouth. "It's not just red," I told her, "It's NDN red." I wondered if that was what Sissy Spacek felt like when she torched her high school gymnasium—it was my Carrie moment.

Both Brooke and I were suspended for the remainder of the week. When I got home and told my mom, I thought she was going to give me a good spanking, but instead she smiled and high-fived me.

I wished with everything I had that the food colouring would stain Brooke's mouth forever, because redness was their lord's way of chastising you.

XXXVIII

By the time I left Tias's place, the sun was bright and beating down—the heat caused my sweat to intermingle with Tias's lovestink. I lit a cigarette to mask the smell. When I turned on my phone, I saw that I had nine requests for a web-show. Hell, I thought, I could top out my funds to get home in a few hours at this rate.

I wondered how my mom was doing.

Someone named MumbaiBoy messaged me asking for a private show. I typed in a kissy emoji and then an angel emoji to reel him in. Every customer wants to think he's taking your purity—that his dick is the first to penetrate and populate your canals. But if you're smart, you can play that against him and earn yourself a few extra bucks. You need to show that you're a tease but also virginal; that you're loveable but also fuckable. These men are all too easy; they're all a bit voyeur and a bit voyageur. They don't want to play doctor with you so much as they want to be the Jacques Cartier of your hipbones.

"Give me twenty?"

"Down to meet?" Mumbaiboy replied.

"For a fifty, yeah."

"Meet me at The Forks."

When I met up with him, he was older than I thought, maybe in his early thirties. His hair and eyebrows were a rich, dark brown and his skin was as dark as mine. His hair was disheveled from the wind blowing in from the Red River. He had deep-set laugh lines and faint crow's feet—for this reason, I figured he was trustworthy. On the rez and in Winnipeg, there was this rivalry between the Indians and us NDNs. Hell, most Nates I knew loved most East Asians; we loved their stories, loved their horoscopes, loved their tea and herbs—but an Asian with a bit of brown was a little competitive, setting up a *West Side Story* kind of turf war. At a house party once, this Filipino boy told us they used pig's blood to boil meat and all the Nates there called it "nasty"; some of them even jeered that it was "right savage." But I always thought, hell, we're not that different, eh? I've eaten the guts of deer and elk before. "Traditional," they'd say, like ceremony was a one-way street.

Mumbaiboy bought us both a round of PBR's at Muddy Waters smokehouse. One of the waiters was trade and I had to avoid making eye contact because he'd been a resource I'd tapped a little too often. But avoiding him was easy when you're two brown boys wearing T-shirts two sizes too small.

"I always had a thing for Indians," Mumbaiboy told me.

I bit my lip. "Yeah, me too," I said in my best Marilyn Monroe voice, even though I don't think either of us knew who we were talking about, at least I didn't.

Afterwards he took me to his apartment, which was down St. James. He said he broke up recently with his girlfriend and that he's been experimenting with boys on hookup apps ever since. He told me his real name, Aric, but I still called him Mumbaiboy.

His apartment was quaint, I guess you'd say. There was no TV. Large black bookshelves filled his living room; all types of books lined his walls: Hemingway, Poe, and interestingly, John Richardson. I remembered reading his book *Wacousta* back in the day. As Mumbai-boy gave me a quick tour, he glossed over his library, telling me that I wouldn't be interested in those boring books, which I found a bit insulting. Then he led me to the bedroom and slowly stripped me of my clothes. He kept his jeans on and left his button-down shirt open, and I could see his nipples harden in the air-conditioned room.

I knelt down in front of him and took hold of his hips. I looked up at him. His eyes were dark and sullen, but they were soft and pleading too. His look was so melancholy that it made me want to cradle him. I wrapped my arms around his waist and he ran his hands through my hair. I sandwiched his leg between my thighs. In my experience, I've found that if you make holes in your body by curling your fingers or contouring your limbs into a shape that's fuckable, a man will always try to fill it.

I could feel his penis harden beneath his jeans.

And just like that something in him awakened too. He pulled me to my feet, threw me on his bed, yanked down his jeans, and fucked me right then and there. I pretended he was Tias. I wondered if I was making love to all the books that lined his shelves; I wondered, if I fuck him back, will my cock puncture the fontanelle of the larger men he's loved and consumed like Hemingway and John Richardson? I wondered, which of us is the *real* Indian?

He lasted maybe five minutes. When his warm cum pooled between my thighs, I felt him release every morsel of breath that he'd been holding in. It sounded more like the noise a television makes when your cable company cuts you off than it did a man.

His eyes refocused on me. "I thought you'd be skinnier," he said. I bit my lip and nodded, then grabbed my fifty and left. How fucked up, I thought. I may not have the best body but I do have *a* body—and it's a body that deserves to be touched and loved and owned, annit?

XXXIX

When we camped out in Hecla, Tias's parents did not let us out of their sight because of our beach night shenanigans. Funny how easy we were to entertain those days; Tias's parents blew up a beach ball and the four of us played "Keep Up" on the gravel road for hours. Whoever was the one to drop the ball had to sit out and the winner got a Starburst candy—save for Tias's dad, who got to take another swig of his beer.

The sun beat down on us as it rose to the top of the sky; the heat became dense. Our skin clung to our cotton t-shirts and sweat pooled in our pits and on the curvature of our spines. My momma said I got that from my daddy—his propensity for sweat. It always embarrassed me. Any bit of heat and I'd be wetter than an otter. All the kids used to make fun of me in school for it: "Jonny, did you just jump out of the pool?" School was excellent practise in learning how to tell stories to finagle myself out of embarrassing situations: "Naw, I wet my hair in the water fountain to keep it looking slick." Sometimes they'd buy it, but the maps my body etched out on my shirts told another story. I still do that, hell, when white people ask where I'm from I can never bring myself to say Peguis or Winnipeg—it doesn't sound exotic enough, doesn't make me seem like I'm more than the sum of my NDN cells. Sometimes I'll say Toronto or Montreal because I've heard those are places where classy people come from. But I'd always pray to Manito that they wouldn't be like, "Oh, whereabouts? I'm from there too" because then I'd really be in deep shit. The only French I ever learned was from watching *Moulin Rouge* whenever it was on TV and I saved that sexy talk for the bedroom: "Hey, Tias? Voulez-vous coucher avec moi ce soir?"

The last time I heard fancy French was when Jordan won a big-ass pot at bingo and took the two of us out to this right nice dinner at the Fort Garry with all these francophone waiters. Tias was back on the rez at the time, and Jordan couldn't bear to be alone, hell, any NDN with a pot that big would never celebrate solo. Everyone said that the Fort Garry was haunted, but there was no scaring an NDN as traditional as Jordan—I was sure she carried sweet grass and an abalone bowl in her purse wherever she went.

"Order whatever you want," she said as we looked at the menu. She was wearing Levi's and a Friendship Centre T-shirt, and I was wearing a pair of blue jeans and an Adidas sweater. I had thought I looked fancy, but I looked around and everyone was wearing a shirt and tie or an expensive-looking dress. I would catch people stealing glances at us, probably wondering what the hell the two of us were doing there. I threw my coat on over top of my sweater, which at least was leather.

"Don't let these môniyâw intimidate you, Jon, fuck 'em," Jordan said.

"I'm not embarrassed, hell, I'm just cold, okay? Lay off." Part of me wanted to tell her I was sorry for lashing out at her instead of them, but I didn't. Jordan had it figured out, though. Whenever someone looked at her, she gave them the evil eye. She hated to be stared at, took it as a sign of disrespect, and responded with an invitation to fight. No one really dared stare at us after that.

Our waiter was a real sexy white man, the kind you hide from your momma after a land claims debate and a secret snag. I ordered pork confit, which I somehow knew how to pronounce, and Jordan ordered a bison tenderloin, along with a $75 bottle of wine. The menu said, "From the land" and I thought to myself, "Yeah right, honey." It reminded me of what we used to eat on the rez: rabbit stew, elk burgers, deer steaks, carrots and onions straight out of the ground, homemade berry jam, Saskatoon pies—the first few weeks after I left the rez, I kept throwing up from all the cheap-ass food I bought from Wal-Mart and McDonald's.

When our food came, Jordan and I looked at each other with a puzzled look—the fuck was this? My pork was so small it looked like there were only four bites' worth, and Jordan's bison was so rare it looked like it was cut straight from the goddamn living animal—did the chef think we were that savage? And forty dollars a plate for this? A hardcore rip-off, if you ask me.

We soon realized we couldn't be white suburban classy. I hated the meal, I wished we were at Neechi Commons instead, but I ate it all save for licking the plate because my kokum told me never to waste good food. We did get dessert with our meal, which was nice; I got a lemon strawberry cake and was super excited to have something I finally liked. But the goddamn thing was the size of a toonie, and I ate it in one bite—the hell, I thought, this is basically the amount of food we put out as an offering to the spirits at a smudge.

"You wanna just dine and dash this bitch?" Jordan asked, eyeing up the joint. I nodded, this meal wasn't worth no damn two bills.

"Okay, I'll stuff my coat into my purse and go for a smoke break," she said. "You wait a minute or two, then go to the bathroom, it's right beside the entrance. Then when you're coming back out, just leave and meet me around back."

"What if they stop me?"

"Say you're coming to get me, easy as pie."

As Jordan got up to leave, I slid my wallet back into my pocket. I started to feel a bit guilty for screwing our cute waiter, but I thought, *You know what? fuck it*, and wrote "Hit me up sometime, cutie" on a napkin alongside my Snapchat handle and a winky face for him to see. When I ran out the door, Jordan was there, and we took off, both wine drunk, running back down Broadway towards The Forks. The smell of the Red was strong tonight—a pungent scent of fish and diesel, the harsh screech of the CPR, the flash of graffiti gang signs. We had both lived out our *Pretty Woman* fantasy that night—but she was the one who was a little more Richard Gere, me a little more Julia Roberts.

Jordan invited me back to her place, so we hopped on the bus on Main Street and headed for the North End. Once there, we downed a few beers.

"Ah fuck it. Wanna just crash here tonight?" she asked.

I didn't feel like stumbling back to the Exchange this late at night— all those bro-dudes thinking they're hot shit eating at the ol' Poutinerie and listening to some shaggy-headed band playing Journey on the second floor of the Kings Head, and me having to make my way through the crowds of drunk Nates wearing ratty coats ripped in the pits.

"Yeah, for sure," I said.

So we logged in to her neighbour's wifi and watched *Zack and Miri Make a Porno* on her VOD. And I guess the wine and beer kicked in, one thing led to another, and we started making out on the couch. Her tongue tasted like cigarettes and Budweiser and her mouth was warm as bathwater. Her arms slid down my back, lifted my shirt up, her fingers feeling the raised scar at the back of my neck. Her nails were sharp as she dug them into my shoulders. Her mouth met my neck and she suckled it like a hungry calf. I moved my hands over her curves from her shoulders down to her breasts, to the sharp indent of her waist.

I slid off her jeans, then her underwear. I kissed my way down to her vagina, her body like a ravine with berry bushes around its perimeter, a cedar trail guiding me to the mound. The folds of skin confused me, but I did as I was taught by the Fishermen boys—counted with my tongue, peyak, niso, nisto, spelled out words like nimis, pîkiskâci, miwâsin. As she moaned I thought of Tias, of how I hadn't seen him naked in a while, of the way his musk always led me to his penis. I discovered how Jordan's body sang with mine, like finding something I had lost.

But as we made stories with each other's bodies, I got a nosebleed. I didn't notice it at first, but when I saw it I panicked—the terrifying sight of seeing my Cree leak out of me, a reminder that "You can die here too." I scrambled from her body's grasp, my face a stained map. For a brief moment we stared at each other, each of our faces distorted with a look of shock that mimicked the other. We both became aware of what we were doing at the same time.

"Get out!" she yelled, looking down at herself, tears meeting blood meeting sweat. "Get the fuck out!"

On the beach, after hours of us playing "Keep Up," Tias's mom cooked us up hot dogs and Kraft Dinner over the fire. By then his dad was getting drunk and talking to their neighbour about his Ford F150. As we waited for supper, Tias started reading a book from school that someone had handwritten "Robert Frost is a fag" on the cover. I decided to draw a picture of our camp. I made steep uphill lines for trees, soft twirls for water, and used heavy pressure to shade in the skin of the boy I knew I loved. I always had trouble drawing his face; there was no amount of lead that could properly detail his features: that low forehead, the concave jut of his cheeks, the bushiness of his unibrow before he learned how to trim it. After dinner, his dad played Johnny Cash on his guitar, his mom cleaned the dishes, and Tias and I sat and stared at a fire that never let up.

When his parents fell asleep, we snuck back to the beach with a handful of sparklers and a few fireworks we smuggled in from the rez. We threw our towels on the sand, ripped off our clothes, and ran into the water that was as shiny as a whale's back. The air was cold but the water was warm; we swam in circles around each other, dipping our heads beneath the water, holding onto each other so we didn't drift off into the darkness. Water always has a way of hiding imperfections— giving my body, still puffy with baby fat in places that shamed me, long lean lines as I dove beneath the surface. And it gave Tias, who already had a beautiful body, muscles that glistened, his skin as tight as a hand drum, penis coming into itself like a mallet.

We got out after what seemed like hours, shivering in the lake wind. We laid on the beach naked, our cocks and balls shriveled into themselves—we must have looked like aliens there, no genitals, just flat, sexless bodies. The night was thick so we lit our sparklers, the flakes of metal flaring between us, touching our skin, burning for a second, leaving marks like hickeys on our chests and legs. Then we kissed, our chins above a heat that scorched our budding hairs, his lips tasting of stale water and crinkled like tinfoil. But our heads fit together without having to twist much. When I bit his lip, my teeth caught some dead skin, which I pulled into my mouth—he tasted like the salty skin of a pickerel.

"The fuck?" he said, pulling away, his lip shiny with a single bead of blood.

"Sorry, man," I said. "My tooth got caught."

Sand had crusted on our bodies, found its way into our bottoms, powdered our scrotums like the Shake-n-Bake that my kokum put on her chicken.

"Don't worry about it, man, but fuck, that hurt," he said, as he wiped himself with the back of his hand and then stared at it. "We should probably get back anyways, y'know?"

We threw on our shorts and tees and wrapped our towels over our heads to dry our hair, but truth be told I thought mine looked like a luxurious war bonnet. On our way back we got lost as we pushed our way through a path Tias called a short-cut, the long arms of branches slapping at us and the sharp needles of thistle weeds underfoot.

"I know the way," Tias said unconvincingly.

"Ekosi," I said.

"You know, I read this poem today," he said while holding two branches apart so I could walk through them. "Basically about this right here. The woods are scary, dark and deep!" he recited, inflecting the final two words to try and scare me—I wasn't scared, but I did pretend to jump to please him. He put his hands on his hips like a confident warrior, but I thought he looked more like a jester than anything. We continued along the path, Tias leading the way like a bulldozer.

"Hey, Tias?" I said, putting my hand on his shoulder. "You never did finish your story from the other night."

He turned around. "Yeah, what about it?"

"Can I hear it?"

He stared at me for a second, then turned his head back and continued down the path. I didn't say anything, just followed close behind him, our gaits matching and hands sometimes smacking into one another. Our feet were beginning to feel bruised, but he said he still knew how to get back. I trusted him, since he came here more often than I did—and there's a kind of safety in letting someone else lead the way. Still, it's funny how your mind plays tricks on you in the dark—everything looks like it's ready to pounce on you, to grab you, to shake and slap you.

The third time our hands bumped together, he grabbed my hand, laced his fingers through mine, pulled me along like a string.

"I have this picture," he said, pulling me in closer, our hips almost aligned. "She's a baby." I didn't want to respond this time, I knew I'd fuck it all up—betray his trust again. I needed to listen fiercely and respond through my body.

"We're sitting together on this lawn, I don't know where it is." I squeeze the meat of his thumb.

"She's sitting between my legs, maybe three months old or something, I'm maybe two?" I continue to squeeze the ball of his hand like they taught me at Camp Arnes.

"She's so goddamn tiny, you know?" Squeeze it like they taught me after we sang "Jonny Appleseed," amen.

"We're just hugging each other. And her fingers are so little and pink. And every time I look at them I see how dark my knuckles are—I know I haven't fought enough in my life for them to be that black, you know?" I'm squeezing SOS into his palm like I'm pressing an orange.

"And then I look at hers and see that hers are not much lighter than mine." I squeeze a different word that Louis the camp counselor taught me with the grinding of his hips into mine, watch Tias's body crumple like a piece of paper in a fire.

"Why were they so dark, Jon, why are they so dark?" Then all of a sudden Tias is hunched over crying and his palm goes limp. I pull him into me, wrap my arms around him like an oyster. I kiss his forehead and he looks up at me, his lashes clumped together from tears.

"Why did I have to lose her too?" he asks. I have no answers for him other than this is the way it is for NDNs—but that's a truth I don't need to repeat to him.

"I think I see it," I say, take both his hands into mine, pull him upright like I'm a powerful ox all of a sudden.

"You know what the fucked-up thing is?" he says, wiping his eyes. "When I showed my parents, they said she looked cute enough to eat. Who the fuck says that?"

I steered the both of us in the direction of the path again and this time I led the way, pulling Tias along with all my might. We didn't say anything else to each other that night, but as I churned those images over and over in my head, I heard him whisper to himself, "Miles to go before I sleep."

XL

I've always been afraid to sleep alone. See, I had a lot of "invisible friends" when I was a toddler. My mom took no notice of it; to her, it was natural for little NDN kido who lived way out in the middle of nowhere to have invisible friends. But one day, I told her, "Mom, Grandpa says hello."

I never met my kokum's first husband, my mother's father. My grandpa's name was Roderick Simpson and he was a beloved hunter on the rez. He used to trap rabbits and sometimes lynx in the summer and skin them for their pelts, then my kokum would cook rabbit stew and make a roast of the occasional lynx that would get caught. My grandpa and kokum became well known for their pelts and dried meats and were popular with the Ukrainian colony that was situated next to the rez; my grandpa would trade them for their chicken eggs and potpies. My grandparents became good friends with the Ukrainians that way—my kokum would always have a chicken potpie from the Ukrainians on hand, ready for company.

My mother freaked out when I told her I saw Grandpa. Not only that, I described him in perfect detail, from his short, thin hair that made his head look like a stippling brush to the crooked twist of his nose. When my mom called Kokum, she came over right away and brought her smudge bowl, tortoise rattle, drum, sweetgrass, and sage to cleanse the house of spirits. I wasn't allowed to watch, so I sat in my room in the basement while they conducted the ceremony.

The basement was always dank and cold. My mother and Kokum's loud footsteps made me shudder, and I could smell the smoke of their medicines. I finally fell asleep listening to the rhythmic shake of my kokum's tortoise rattle. When it was over, both women came downstairs to wake me and told me that I wouldn't be bothered by spirits anymore.

But around this same time, I began to see a lot of shadows in the basement—which could have been caused by the swaying ceiling light, or from what I would later learn to call the "little people."

I had a lot of night terrors.

Because of this, I slept with my mom almost every night for a year, much to Roger's dismay. I never ventured downstairs to my bedroom save for a fresh pair of clothes and the odd chore for my mother. On occasions when I did, I would turn on all the lights and run back upstairs as quickly as I could. To help me with my anxieties, Roger concocted a plan. He told me a story of the mannegishi.

"When I was a boy," he said softly, "I used to see little people too. I always saw them jumping down from the ceiling light in my room in the basement. Used to spook my mom out so much that one time when I saw a shadow run across the wall and screamed, my mom pushed me out of her way and ran upstairs. We were all afraid of them. But my gran told me that it was a blessing to see the mannegishi. They say that only children and medicine people can see them. And if you treat them right and offer them tobacco, they're supposed to help you. They're super hairy and ugly—so don't look them in the face. But they're little, very little, and like to play tricks on people. That's probably why they're bugging you." Then he pulled out a handful of jelly beans from his pocket. "We'll use these," he said, "to get them to ease up on their tricks."

He led me by the hand to my basement bedroom. We searched the room from top to bottom. We pulled out my drawers, checked in the pockets of my sweaters, hell, Roger even unscrewed the vents to peer into them with his flashlight. We didn't find any mannegishi.

"See, little people, they love shiny things," Roger said. "My gran told me that. She said that you can never get rid of them, that they follow families around when they move. So we're stuck with these damned little annoying fucks!" He was half-shouting, half laughing. "She told me that if you can offer them treats, they'll usually leave you alone. This is what I always did." Then he pulled out a crumpled bit of tinfoil and placed it on the floor. He unfolded it, shaped it into a little bowl, and placed the jelly beans inside. "This here tinfoil will attract them. They'll take the jelly beans as an offering. To them, in the spirit world, a jelly bean is like the equivalent of receiving an entire elk—a little goes a long way. They'll be full and sugar-high for a while yet. Give them more in a few months and you'll be okay, Jonny."

Together we placed the tinfoil bowl of jelly beans beneath my bed and we went upstairs, where my mom made us hot chocolate, and then we all sat down and watched *Family Feud*. That night, I slept in their bed straight through till morning, when Roger and I went to check on our tinfoil trap. To our astonishment, the jelly beans were gone. It never occurred to me that maybe my mom or Roger himself woke up in the middle of the night to eat those jelly beans—as far as I knew, they were gone to the spirit world. I had fewer nightmares after that, fewer visions of shadows running across the walls. And fewer hangouts with Roger.

My kokum told me once that the mannegishi are helpers to medicine people—that she too had seen them and asked them for help. She joked that this was how she found all of her keys that she had once lost. When I told my kokum of my dreams, she let me talk and would listen carefully, nodding gently while sipping her tea. "Some people think their name means hairy—that they're ugly and mean spirits," she finally said. "But from my experience, m'boy, they're quite nice. Other people say that their name means butterfly, from the Ojibwe word memengwaa. Maybe that's what they are to you, m'boy? Butterflies."

It reminded me of this poem we read in school once, by John Keats, who said that he wished he were a butterfly and lived only three short days—and he would fill those three short days with more delight than fifty common years could contain. Since my conversation with my kokum that day, I've always thought of my relationship with the spirit world along those lines, that the mannegishi and the dreams they gave me showed me that I was a pupa and the rez my chrysalis; that I was living on borrowed time and that my three short days had a deadline—but hey, it's like I always say: what's three days in regular time is five in NDN time.

XLI

I walked from St. James to Ellice and then caught a cab for the rest of the way home—I just made fifty dollars, I thought, so spending ten isn't going to ruin my trip. It figures I'd forget my keys at Tias's place so that I'd have to break into my own home, Native Problems 101. Every NDN I've ever met has devised several methods to do this. Mine was asking my neighbour if I could shimmy from his balcony to mine, where I always left a window unlocked. And if my neighbour wasn't home, I let myself in using the key he hid in the nook beneath his door—he never seemed to mind.

When I finally got inside, my phone was blinking with messages from more clients; this time I had an additional three unread messages. That meant twelve clients. If each averaged twenty dollars a pop for a webcam peek-a-boo, at roughly twenty minutes per session, then I could, if my body were up to it, earn up to 240 dollars today. That would put me well over the amount it would take to get back home to the rez; that is, if I could only stop spending money on cigarettes, Big Bites, and cab rides when I still needed to top off my rent for the month and pay back Ernie for his weed.

I figured I'd call my mom to see how she's doing before I began my all-night webcam sessions. Her cellphone was cut off because the outstanding bill on her landline was hefty, so I resorted to the old-school NDN method of instant messaging. I picked up the phone and dialed her collect; when the operator asked me to state my name, I fit in as many words as I could: "Hi Mom, it's Jonny, how's things on your end—" Beep. The operator cut me off and rang my mom. On the sixth ring, I heard her answer, "Hello?" and the automated answer of, "You have a collect call from: Hi Mom, it's Jonny, how's things on your end—beep." I heard her laugh. I then hung up so she could collect-call-instant-message me back. This was how we used to talk all the time, when neither of us had a penny to put on our MTS phone bills.

When my phone rang, I quickly picked it up. "You have a collect call from: Hey babe, I've been better when you coming—beep."

"You have a collect call from: Should be there tomorrow, low on funds—beep."

"You have a collect call from: You better get your scrawny ass here, boy—beep."

"You have a collect call from: I will, Momma, promise—beep."

"You have a collect call from: Mmkay m'boy, make sure you d— beep."

"You have a collect call from: Pinky swear, love you—beep."

I had twenty-four hours to do ten webcam shows, earn another 200 bucks, pack, sleep, and find myself a ride for the four-hour drive to Peguis.

In addition to the three missed phone calls, there was a text message from Tias: "Where'd you go? I want to talk to you about something."

A part of me wished that Jordan had a landline too—the harsh clank of a thrown-down receiver was the aural equivalent of a slap to the face. It was the best way to tell a person to fuck off without having to say the words. I texted him back with a simple, "No." I made an emphasis to punctuate my text. In the digital universe, a punctuated sentence is as powerful a slap as slamming down the landline.

I knew what was coming, heck, it was the same-old-same-old routine any couple of NDN breeders went through, on or off the rez, salmon patch and all.

It was going to be a long night.

XLII

When we were kids, all my cousins and I used to visit my kokum's house every day. I loved playing with the mangy rez dogs that hung around her home. She always kept a large bag of dog kibble and had each of us scoop out bowlfuls for the dogs that came to her porch hungry. And she had a large field in front of her house where they'd wrestle, fuck, sleep, and shit. I spent far too much time in that field sweet-talking dogs that never called me weird or faggot. Truth be told, I was afraid of men and I learned a lot about my masculinity by playing with those dogs.

The men in my family often tried to teach me practical skills like how to use tools, start a fire, hunt, and skin animals. I never had an aptitude for many of these, hell, whenever I built a piece of furniture from Wal-Mart it always seemed inevitable that I would build it backwards three times, get mad, and then leave it like that. The end table in my apartment has three unfinished edges that I've coloured over with black sharpie to hide the flaws. I may not be a goddamned carpenter or a hunter, but let me tell you, I'm crafty as all hell.

I always preferred having female teachers, friends, and guidance counselors. The men in my life liked to pressure me to butch myself up and ridicule me for my feminine ways. When I was in the fourth grade, my school had a Halloween dance. I wanted to be Minnie Mouse, but Roger wouldn't let me buy a girl's costume—instead, he bought me the Mickey Mouse version. Before going to the party, my kokum made me a makeshift bow, then she painted my face up like a mouse, adding her blush to my cheeks and mascara to my lashes. I felt like Minnie in that moment and that was enough for me.

No one at the party seemed to care about what any of us were wearing. I remember a lot of dreadfully tacky fabrics and *Scream* masks. When "Ghostbusters" started playing, Shane, my only friend at the time, asked me to dance. He put his left hand on my hip and his right clasped my left hand, and we waltzed around the room to Ray Parker Jr.'s exhortations. That was the first time I'd ever touched a boy beyond the exchange of chest bumps or pats on the back.

When I got home and excitedly told my kokum what had happened, she laughed and patted me on the arm, and my mom reacted in much the same fashion. But Roger, overhearing our excitement, unbuckled his belt, pulled it out of its loops, and doubled it over in his hands like a bullwhip. He grabbed me by the back of my shirt collar, bent me over the table, pulled down my underwear, and gave me one hell of a lickin while my kokum and mom yelled for him to stop.

"Boys don't"—*smack*—"dance with"—*smack*—"boys"—*smack*.

The sound of his leather belt slapping against the bare skin of my ass crackled throughout the house. I imagined the rez dogs in the front yard lowering their ears, hiding in the long grass, and whimpering. My flesh reddened and began to split. Roger had broken the skin and I could feel a tiny dabble of blood trickling between my cheeks.

When his arms got tired, he commanded that I "get out of his sight." I ran to my bedroom, locked the door, and inspected the marks on my bottom in the mirror. They were tender and throbbing. It hurt, but I had to admit, a part of me was excited too.

I took off my pants and lay on the carpet on my stomach. I rested the cool side of my pillow on my ass. That's when I discovered the sensations my body could produce. I dragged my pelvis across the carpet and learned how good I could make myself feel by rubbing my lump of flesh.

Not only was that my first encounter with Roger's mean streak, but it was also the awakening of my queer body. The trickle of blood, the splitting of skin, the pain on my ass cheeks, the full-body pleasure of an ejaculation—I felt as new as those rare trees split wide open after a storm, all tender and wondrously ravaged.

XLIII

I have a deep-set belly button that everyone made fun of when I was a kid. I was a chubby boy and whenever we went swimming, I always hesitated to take off my shirt. When I did, my aunties would tell me to run slowly towards them along the rapids. "You're like on *Baywatch*," they'd yell, pointing to the jiggle of my stomach fat. But it was my belly button that entertained them the most. It must have been an inch deep. My uncles would take their flashlights to inspect my belly's flesh-cavern and yell, "Helllllooooo!" I always wondered, were they looking for a baby in there?

When we had swimming lessons at school, I asked Roger to write me a note to excuse me from P.E. When I told him I was afraid to swim, he sat me on his lap.

"What's bugging you?"

I told him of the shame I felt when I was naked; how the other boys would whip me with their towels and poke at my fatty rolls. And they were drawn to my freak belly button too—the large, gaping hole that wobbled like a grape inside those gross old jello salads. Roger balled my hand into a fist and raised it to the hollow between his eyes.

"You see this spot right here?" he said. "Whenever someone's bugging you, well, you hit them right here and they'll go straight down. And if they don't, their eyes will be tearing up so much that you can swing another hit or two and finish 'em off."

Roger had a way of thinking he was the NDN Rocky Balboa—he was always offering brawling techniques to others. I've seen him fight a few times; he had a goofy yet terrifying look to him when he was angry. He was known as "Sucker Punch Smiley" by his friends because whenever he was sizing up a would-be opponent, he would smile at them. And it would always catch his enemies off guard—while they were trying to figure out his demeanor, Roger would sucker punch them with an uppercut to the chin. It worked every time. And since Roger had such a large clan of cousins on the rez, no one ever tried to jump in for fear of his family's retaliation. He was smart in that regard. He may not have been a world-class boxer, but boy, for a scrawny, 150-pound NDN, he had no problems taking down a man twice his size.

Roger lifted up his shirt and pointed to the large ash-coloured scar that ran horizontally across his waist. "See this?" he said. "Here's where I had my kidney removed a few years back." And then he pointed to three little scars that formed a triangle on his abdomen: one between his ribcage, one on his right side, and one in his belly button. "See this one? Had my gallbladder removed, too." There were stories for each of the scars on his body—some from surgeries, some from sicknesses, some from scrapping—stories that I've heard him rehash a million times. He had survived cancer, a few overdoses, and had even been stabbed before—but he was still trucking along. At least he was then.

It was the scar inside his belly button that always caught my attention. One time he let me touch the raised ridge of skin. "Does it hurt?" I asked.

"The gallstones? Fuck, yeah. But the wound? Nah. Not anymore."

Roger always let me explore his body to appease my own anxieties. His was like a graveyard of injuries and ailments, so alive with experiences, while mine was just riddled with shame. Roger knew the fun my aunties liked to make at my body's expense. And when he sensed that I was worried about my appearance, he'd tell me the story of the belly button that his mother told him before she passed on.

Roger is a Lakota, unlike my mother, who is Cree, so his stories always differed from ours. But I liked what he had to tell us. When he had his gallbladder removed as a kid, his mother told him the importance of his belly button. His people call it the chik'sa and revere it as a sacred body part.

"The chik'sa," Roger said, "is a very important part of our spirituality. They say that the belly button is where the spirits live. You see, when we're born, our moms would take our belly button and place it inside of a turtle shell and then wrap both of those in a buckskin satchel. And they'd safeguard it for their baby until they were old enough to have it. Do you know why?"

I shook my head.

"Because the turtle always returns to his birthplace. So, when my mom put my belly button inside of the turtle shell, she was combining us spiritually—you know? It was so that I'd always know how to come home if I ever got lost or left."

"And did you?"

"Nah—too busy on the warpath," he said, laughing.

A few years after Roger told me that story, I got a wood tick in my belly button. Heck, I didn't know it was a wood tick right away and

I'm not sure how long it had been in there fattening up with blood, but when I stuck my fingers inside, I felt it squirming around. It didn't feel rough or patchy like a wood tick usually does; it was slick, cool, and moist to the touch. In fact, if I had to compare it to anything, I'd say it felt like a watermelon seed. And for an entire week I let it live there, cradling my stomach at night thinking that Manito had gifted me with a watermelon baby to carry and care for.

When I was convinced that it was growing, I told my mom and Roger as they were watching contestants on *The Price Is Right* spin the wheel.

"Guys, I'm having a baby!" I yelled.

They looked perplexed until I lifted up my shirt and showed them the fat, black seed that had filled my belly button. My mother screamed and Roger ran to the kitchen to grab a pair of tweezers. My mom slapped me upside the head and said, "Boy, you're something, you know? That's a damned wood tick, for godsakes."

Roger carefully inserted the tweezers inside and clasped them tightly on the tick. It hurt us both—I could feel the parts of my belly button where my skin had begun to fuse with the tick; my innards felt like a slick, wet olive. Roger then bore down on the tweezers and finally yanked the tick from my belly. I gasped in pain and grasped the couch as blood shot out from the hole, oozed down my navel, and soaked into my underwear. Roger stood over me with the tweezers, the tick still squirming. Afterwards he took that wood tick and held it in his ashtray, then poured salt on it and burned it with his ashes. It died violently, to say the least.

And that's sometimes the strangest thing about pain, that sites of trauma, when dressed after the gash, can become sites of pleasure. Sometimes when he's getting me off, Tias will probe that gaping hole with his forefinger, swab it like a Q-Tip, little excavating NDN always wanting inside of me. And when he has me teetering on that blue-balled edge, I ask myself when I'm about to come just where it is that I'm going?

XLIV

My body was sore from the webcam sessions. I was laying back on my bed and smoking a cigarette, fingering the edges of my belly button. My Snapchat piggy bank said I had $260, and combined with the forty I had left from Mumbaiboy and the funds I made the other day, I had about $420 in total. That would be enough to top up my rent and get my ass to the rez. I figured I'd give ol' Peggy a call and see if she'd run me to the rez for $300; maybe I could even swindle her into giving me a cheaper price.

I had one more day to get there. I figured if I left early enough tomorrow, I could get there by late afternoon. There was enough time, I thought, as I stared up at my stucco ceiling that looked like bat droppings. I opened the blinds and saw that it was dark outside. The streets of Winnipeg were alit with fluorescents, and the Exchange was quiet save for a few rowdy gangbangers I could see hustling in the alleys. There was a line of taxis waiting for fares along Princess Street. Part of me wanted to celebrate, to yell at someone down on the street to come up and toke with me, but no one was around; even my pigeon neighbour was fast asleep in his nest of bones.

I opened my phone and saw that it was 11:27 p.m. Tias had messaged me a couple times. I texted him back: "Hey you want to come over?" I knew I only had to wait maybe twenty minutes, ten if he had cab money or his bike, for him to show up at my door—but only in NDN time. And what was a few minutes more for that inevitable break-up talk? Sometimes I feel like I should have been born a

Cormac, always hitting the road and telling myself, "You can't stop what's coming."

When Tias arrived, he was wearing a band tee and dirty jeans; his breath smelled of Budweiser and his eyes were beginning to glaze over. His lips were crusted with tobacco and roach crumbs. But he flashed the boyish smile that I had come to adore. "Listen, Jonny," he said as he stepped inside and grabbed my arm to look into my eyes. His other hand held onto one of the empty loops of an eight-pack of Bud. I couldn't concentrate, looking down at his boxers peeking out from his jeans.

"Jonny, I need to tell you—"

I grabbed him by the waist, took a beer, and motioned for him to sit down. He closed the door behind him and plopped himself down on the couch. I ripped open the can of Bud and felt the cold sensation of it sliding down my throat as I shotgunned the entire beer in front of him.

"Slow down, Vac," he said, laughing. He patted the seat beside him and unhooked another beer. He passed it to me as I sat down.

"What is it?" I asked.

His lips quivered as if he were bench-pressing too large a weight. And he could lift his weight and then some—I've seen him do it. We used to say we were going to get jacked like the NDN boys we saw on television, like Taylor Lautner or Booboo Stewart.

"You see—"

We'd pick up dumbbells, his in the high twenties and mine in the low teens, and curl them in front of each other. Our veins rose and plumped thick as tree roots. He always teased me for needing a spotter. Sure, I was weak—what do you expect of me? I'd say. My arms are thin as roots and I usually only use them to swatch glosses and liquid lipsticks. But when I did lift that bar on my own, which was only once, Tias cheered and slapped me on my thigh, which made me instantly get hard. I was always full of tricks.

"You know, Jordan and me—"

Tias had a ravenous hunger for sex; he had a lot of fucked-up problems, but god, his body, in pain, turned me on to no end. He suffered so delightfully—and then again, maybe I did too. We fucked right there in his foster family's basement. We hid ourselves by making a fort from old towels held up against the edges of his water heater and dryer. He pushed his tongue so deep down into my throat that it felt more like a dental extraction than love-making, all chase, all coming.

"Jonny, are you even listening?"

He used to hurt me a lot back then, when I didn't know how to let him inside me without clenching my bottom so tightly that his flesh tore into mine. Our bodies were made of cells that were braided together, and particles of blood, semen, and shit that leaked and oozed out from us—bits of discharge that were both living and dying.

"I got her pregnant, Jon." He paused, staring me in the eye. "She's pregnant, Jonny, and I don't know what to do." And then he collapsed in on himself like a piece of plastic burning in a bonfire.

I vacuumed the beer I had in my hand and cracked another.

"Well, shit," I said.

XLV

When I first moved to Winnipeg, Tias never shamed me for leaving Peguis, never called me a traitor, an apple, or a fraud for abandoning my people back home. Heck, I think he was even a little proud of me for leaving; my kokum had just died, and the rez didn't feel like a home anymore. I stayed in bed and slept all day, every day, save for the few times I got up to take a piss or roll a joint. My body was a dead zone. My kokum had always told me that sleep was not a waste of time, that it was a time for healing, so I slept long and hard, waiting for my blood to leech out its memories and for my body to rejuvenate.

In those first few days after I moved to Winnipeg, Tias stuck by me after driving me down there; he took care of me as he helped me settle into my first place in the North End. He set up all my furniture and shooed me away when I tried to help. He wasn't much of a chef but he did keep me fed. He cooked the only food he knew how to make: perogies. I watched him scurry around in the kitchen from the mattress on my floor. He rolled out the dough, cut it into circles with a plastic cup, peeled and boiled potatoes he got from the food bank down the street, and mashed it all together with cheese strings and onion soup mix. Then he delicately poured a spoonful of filling into each circle of dough, folded it over, and pinched it closed with his fingers. They were odd little perogies, all different sizes, and some burst open in the boil—but they sure tasted good. "I'm not sure how a little Nate like me got good at making perogies," he said.

We ate those perogies every day during my first few weeks in Winnipeg. They reminded me of home and my dear departed kokum, though I knew my world was about to change.

XLVI

Tias stayed the night. When I woke up, I decided not to tell him that I was headed back to the rez. The sun was rising and beating down through my blinds. I traced his body with my forefinger as he lay sleeping: from his chest that slowly rose and fell, to the bottom of his rib cage, to the round rise of his hips. I put my ear to his navel, half expecting to hear something, before slipping my tongue inside, wanting to taste Nanaboozho's elixir. Tias woke up and looked down at me.

Without a word we took each other in our mouths, ending with a final plume of cum that slid between our pressed bodies. We didn't bother wiping ourselves, just laid on our backs, his hand in mine, both of us staring at the ceiling and breathing in the hay-scented air.

"We're going to keep it, Jon."

I pressed my thumb into the ball of his hand. I wanted to feel the ridges on his palm, see if his lines were still broken like mine. Where mine were cracked and frayed, his made an "M" shape that took up his entire hand. I brought his hand to my face and I could still smell the beer and cigarettes.

"I've been working on finishing my grade twelve, you know, bettering myself and shit."

I curled my body around his left side, and his arm pulled me in closer.

"And you haven't been around all that much lately, you know?"

I could feel my phone vibrating beneath the pillow. I pulled it out and saw the yellow glow from a new client—Manito, I prayed, give me the strength not to check my Snapchat right now.

"Did you hear what I said? We're going to keep the baby."

I nodded into his armpit and pulled him in tighter. I inhaled his stink and then licked him—I wanted to taste him, consume him, remember him. We wrapped our arms and legs around each other, our heads burrowed into the other's neck like an ouroboros, as tears started streaking down our faces. We used to love holding each other like this—we even made our own verb to describe it: burritoing. "Want to burrito?" he'd ask, and we'd link together and fall asleep that way.

"The world breaks everyone," Tias whispered into my ear. "And after, well, heck, those that make it through are strong at the broken places." He ran his fingers through my hair and lightly grazed my neck with his lips. "Hemingway," he said with pride. "I have to read him for my GED. You should read him sometime."

I nodded and pushed my head against the curve of his fingers.

"I'm gonna finish and get myself straight, Jon. You know, learn a trade or something, for the baby and Jordan and shit."

He kissed my forehead and got out of the bed. The sun was rising higher in the sky, heading toward noon.

"I guess this is goodbye, eh?" he asked, putting on his shirt.

"You mean ekosi?"

"I mean, you don't say!" he laughed.

I smiled and nodded. My pigeon friend was stirring outside my window, flapping its wings awake. Someone was pushing a shopping cart down the back alley, its rickety wheels scraping the pavement.

"Kihtwâm?" he asked.

"Ekosi," I replied.

He unlatched the door and looked back at me. His eyes were full of regret—*there*, I thought, there's the Tias I know. When I tried to kiss him one last time, he turned his head. My lips met the brisk hairs on his neck.

"The rain won't make any difference," I said.

"What?" he said, looking confused, but I closed the door without responding. When I heard his footsteps disappear down the hallway, I went back to bed and checked my phone. I ignored the client requests and saw that Peggy said yes, she'd be here at noon. It was ten o'clock now so I had two hours to pack. But all I wanted to do was stay between these sheets and forget.

I breathed in Tias's scent that he had left on my pillowcases. I guess I was happy for him, Tias could make a home here in Winnipeg—him and his books. I still wasn't sure that what I had was truly mine. All I had was this bed, this wad of bills—and these cum stains on my sheets, this pool of ectoplasm that proclaimed, "We were here."

XLVII

I had this one client, tomass202, a Nate twink with an overbite whose teeth looked like shovels. He said he found my name in the bathroom stall in Peguis Central. We chatted for a month before he started asking for shows. He never asked me to dress up, just asked me to talk to him, then take off my clothes slowly, and while I did to describe my body like it was a portrait painting. "This nipple here, this the one that's extra sensitive," I'd tease, "and if you kiss me here, on the bits of my thigh that look like Kentucky Fried, well, you'll just have to find out—" He was bashful, fidgety, inflamed, but coy. He wore a bandanna to conceal his face, and he kept his hair pulled back in two braids that were hidden by his baseball cap. Took me a while to get him to take off that bandanna: "You ain't gotta hide yourself like it's a graveyard, m'boy." There were too few occasions where I could bedazzle boys with that euphemism; I knew it coaxed Nates like the bad magic my kokum used to tell me about.

We corresponded in short bursts for some time. He asked me questions like I was a goddamn psychiatrist and I kept responding long enough to hear that little "ka-ching" noise of more money going into my account.

"Wut iz it lik3?" he typed in the chat box.

"What's what like?" I responded into the mic.

"Sex," he typed. "It hurt?"

"Nah." I paused. "Nah, it ain't that bad."

"????"

It don't hurt as much as the rest does, I wanted to say, but I closed the chat prematurely.

After about a month of little chats and strip shows, we ended up finally meeting. He said he could host, as his roommates were out shopping in the city for the weekend. When I got to his place, he was only wearing boxers and a ratty wife-beater, and wasted no time dragging me to his bedroom. He shimmied out of his shorts and pulled his shirt up over his chest, and I swear I damn near saw every organ in his body, he was that skinny. I took off my clothes too, and then we laid on his bed facing each other, inspecting one another's body.

We jerked each other off until we got hard, then he climbed on top of me and kneaded his junk against me; he rubbed so damn hard against me that I wondered if he thought our bodies were kindling. "Slow," I said. "Hold onto me tighter, but be patient, like you're fishing or something." He nodded and started to kiss me. His teeth dug into my lip like it was a flowerbed. He kept forgetting to let us breathe so I had to take in large puffs of air whenever I had the chance. I slid his hands over my hips, down to where I needed loving, but he shook his head and lay back down on the bed.

"Can you top me?" he asked. I was taken aback. No one had ever asked me that before, but his face was so goddamn woebegone that I nodded yes. I slid myself between his legs, ran my fingers down his back. When I circled my finger around him, he gasped, and when I slowly slid my fingers inside, he squirmed like a fish on bait. He jolted and I jumped, surprised at how much I could do, but he kept nodding and said, "Keep going." And we worked around one another like that for a while, his eyes growing large at the little world opening for him down there, and me scared of how much power he was granting me. And when I finally entered him, his whole body shook. He wrapped his legs around me like a basket. I thought, *This is it? All of this is the power of man?* It took the entirety of two minutes for me to spill myself over him, two minutes of prayer to Manito that I didn't slip out and fuck up. He finished himself off, a hot sweaty mess, but his body was brown like mine in all the right spots.

"That was, that was—"

"It was," I said.

We cleaned ourselves up with a tube sock and then sat up in the bed, both of us staring out the window. The night was thick and we could hear frogs croaking out of sync with one another.

"You want a smoke?" I asked and he nodded, probably thinking it was *the* thing to do after sex, annit?

I got up and got my smokes, with the intention of stepping outside. "Hold on," he said. "We should put something on, someone will see us."

"Ah for fucksakes, ain't no one out there, it's dark as shit."

I opened the door and we stepped outside naked, the wind splashing against our skin, pushing our testicles back up inside ourselves. I lit us both a smoke and passed him one. I inhaled as deep as I could, tried to burn out that authority wherever it lay deep down in me. He inhaled and coughed, trying to smoke the cigarette like a joint. I rolled my eyes. "Slow," I said again. "You ain't always gotta be rushing everything, m'boy." And there that phrase was again, "m'boy," knocking against my gut like a sledgehammer. He took a deep puff and let it out—there, I thought, now you're getting it. The smoke slithered up into the night sky.

"Do you think I'm sexy?" he asked.

"I think—" I paused to take a drag. "I think you're beautiful for a boy who lets himself feel."

I didn't have the heart to tell him everything, didn't have the courage to say, man, feeling like that's going to break you if you ain't careful.

"It's my first time, y'know," he said, as if I didn't know. "I hope I didn't do anything wrong. Did I make any mistakes?"

"Mistakes?" I tried hard not to laugh. "Well, let's see, your first mistake was asking that." Then I put my hands on his shoulders and pressed my forehead against his. "And your second one was you thinking you ever owed me a goddamn thing."

He nodded, took another drag. "I feel you," he said.

We went back inside and got dressed, his walk now a hearty swagger.

"You staying over?" he asked.

"Nah man, I gotta go. But this was fun."

"Yeah, bro, it really was. We'll have to do it again sometime?"

"Yeah—maybe."

He looked disappointed. He walked me to the door, then gave me a kiss that was more of an attempt at swallowing me whole than a light peck goodbye.

As I opened the door to leave, he grabbed my arm. "Hey, you got any advice for someone like me?" he asked.

"Advice?" I paused for a minute, unable to believe any sad sucker wanted advice from me, the self-ordained NDN princess. "Um, yeah. How about this: we all got thick skin, but we still gotta let people in." I turned to leave, not waiting to see what his response was, because if I did, I knew I'd only see myself looking back at me. Hell, I was never good at tasting my own medicine. I walked home thinking of him and our strange date. For a minute I was convinced his was a body I could love, but I fit into him in all the wrong places. Advice? What kind of bullshit was that? Hell, you want some advice, boy? Here's some straight from me to you: *use those teeth—use 'em to dig yourself out of every ass you eat.*

XLVIII

Peggy picked me up forty minutes late. Her hair was a bundle of auburn curls that reminded me of Barbra Streisand in *A Star Is Born*. Her van was rezzed out and dirty as all hell; I wondered, how does she even see out of this mopbucket? I handed her the money; she agreed to $250, which left me fifty to spend on a few packs of cigarettes and a handful of Twizzlers from Mac's. We made good time leaving the city; we would be in Peguis come nightfall if we kept up this pace. Peggy drove like a bat out of hell, weaving between traffic as we sped by lakeside beaches and small towns.

At one point, she asked, "Stop-at-Saltys-for-a-dog-er-what?"

"Maybe next time, Peg, I gotta make that funeral, you know."

"Pfft-boy-you're-slack-but-yeah-eh-okay-you're-right-let's-go." She stuck out her tongue with a pop and let out a "Mlaaa." Every time she did that, I laughed. My kokum was notorious for doing the same thing.

I dozed off at some point, but when we passed by Narcisse, Peggy roused me awake.

"Eh-you-think-these-here-snakes-can-crawl-up-through-our-wheels-if-we-run-them-over?"

"Huh?"

"You-think-these-snakes-will-curl-up-in-the-wheelwell-and-bite-our-ankles-later?"

I just nodded because I was too tired to ask her to explain.

She frowned at me and laughed to herself anyways. "You-know-like-*Snakes-on-a-Plane*?"

The sun was setting as Peggy's car lights flashed on the Welcome to Peguis sign. I couldn't believe I was back.

As we drove past St. Peter's cemetery, I waved hello to my kokum.

The entrance to the rez has always had a sign that read: "Peguis First Nation welcomes you" and lists the names of the chief and council. When I used to live there, the chief was Louis Stevenson. The last time I tried to visit the rez, there was a terrible rainstorm and the sign had fallen over. The road was washed out so we could only make it to the entrance. All I saw was a brown horse standing by itself on a small patch of land completely surrounded by water. Its belly was fat and I wondered how in the hell a horse could still be well fed and placid in a drowning world.

I never made it back to the rez that day. The ride I was in was forced to turn around on account of the flooding and as it did, I watched the horse slowly disappear in the rear window. My eyes were locked on a white spot on his lower thigh until he became a brown blur in a blue glaze.

Nowadays I say "holy hell" every time I think of home.

"She-was-a-good-woman-your-kokum," Peggy said. "I-known-her-a-long-time, always-smiling, always-happy, and-she-loved-you-like-crazy."

I nodded in agreement. Peggy had a pretty famous grandma on the rez too, named Evelyn. Both our grandmothers shared the sugar disease, they were both diabetic. And Evelyn, well, she loved her brown sugar. My kokum used to say that Evelyn would come over for breakfast with a pot of Cream of Wheat and a big bag of sugar. She'd warm up her cereal in the microwave and serve them both a bowl. Evelyn would top hers with even more milk and then meticulously add a layer of brown sugar. She'd wait for it to melt into a brown glaze before eating it, adding even more sugar as she made her way through the bowl. Often, my kokum told me, Evelyn would use up a good third, if not half, of the bag.

"But I never stopped her," my kokum said. "That cereal was hers to enjoy. Know why? Those priests, they used to only feed her Sonny Boy when she was in them schools."

"How-long-you-been-gone-anyways?" Peggy asked.

"Maybe couple years now?"

"Holy-hell-that's-long."

I lost count how many times we said "holy hell" on the drive in. And I got to thinking that us NDNs say "holy hell" so damned much because we figured out how to live and love in the holy hell of apocalyptic shitstorms.

When we finally got to my mom's trailer, I gave Peggy a big hug and thanked her for the ride.

"Maybe you should use some of the money I gave you to wash your car," I said, pointing at the dust on her back windows. She laughed.

"You-wanna-come-to-a-party-tonight-before-things-get-serious?"

"Nah, Peg, I'm good. Be safe, okay?"

She nodded, then put her car in reverse and drove back down the gravel highway. I knew she'd spend most, if not all, of that money on booze tonight. Hell, she'd probably end up stranded here too. I started to feel bad for bringing her back. As I walked up to my mom's door, there were two cars rusting in the yard, tire rims scattered on the porch along with kid's toys, dog food, and empties.

I was back, and the whole damn rez looked, felt, even smelled the same. All my cousins were still here, for the most part. Maybe Nates stay on the rez because they've been pushed so far already. But wherever we end up, we can take pride in knowing that we can survive where no one else can, and that we can make a home out of the smallest of places, and still be able to come home and say, "I love you, Mom."

I knocked on Momma's front door thinking about her, wondering if she was a lightning-struck tree like me, all rare and beauteous in our pain. I hoped she would give me that slap upside the head, reel me into her weathered arms, and speak to me in that old-fashioned Cree, kisâkihitin, m'boy, kisâkihitin, and tell me stories of how we've lived, and loved, and grown.

XLIX

She thought I wasn't coming.

When my mom opened her front door, she took hold of my whole body and lifted me off the ground in a huge bear hug. Her grip had gotten stronger since I'd last seen her. Her hair was in a messy ponytail and she wasn't wearing any makeup, but her face looked exactly as I remembered it: hard and aged, but kind.

"You missed the wake," she said.

"I know, Mom, I'm sorry. I didn't have the cash to return sooner, you know, shit, that old rez money don't reach that far off the rez. But I'm here now, right? Solid as a rock."

"We still have so much left to do. We have to help Mabel make the dainties for the service, I still have to pick up the flowers for Roger, and I still have no idea what the fuck I'm going to wear—"

I grabbed her and hugged her tightly again.

"I'll help you with all of that," I said. "Are you okay?"

"Babe, heck, I just missed you."

We held each other like that for a while, then she made us tea and ripped us a slab of bannock, which we sloppily slathered with butter and jam.

"I was in hell," she said in between bites. "Straight up hell, Jon." I wanted to say me too, tell her ain't nothing straight about hell, but instead I sliced another piece of bannock in two. "He ain't ever tell me it got that bad, fucking asshole," she said. I used my fork to pull the tub of margarine towards me, slid my knife into it. "Who the hell does that? Who in their right mind peaces out leaving their nicîmos like that? Fucking dumb-ass, he'd go out with all those cousins of his, day in, day out; wake up, sip, get dressed, sip, go out, sip, come home, sleep—repeated that shit every day." I didn't say anything, just kept spreading the margarine hard across the two bannock halves, spilling crumbs everywhere. "I know I ain't no saint, Jon, I know I been friends with that old bottle too damn long too—but, I only ever do it to whittle time, at least that's what I told myself." I spread the raspberry puree on the bannock next, that dark red jam oozing into the newly formed crevices. "And each time he'd come back I'd see how time etched into him, his muscles became sandbags. His calves were thin enough for me to wrap my fucking hand around. And his whole body went yellow as piss." I took a bite from one half of the bannock and slid the other half across to her. "He looked like a goddamned skeleton, Jon, my old man was walking around dead as a doornail." She shook her head, pushed the bannock aside.

"And he tells me, Karen, ain't nothing no hospitals gonna do, fuck, I go there with strep throat and they ask me, 'You drunk, boy?' Ain't nothing they gonna do, ain't no one gonna give a liver to an NDN whose already punched out." Momma's curls fell across her face, hiding her, but her eyes peeked through, making her look feral, wounded, sad as a fox stuck in a hunter's trap. "Said to me, 'Karen, it's my time—ain't nothing wrong with that,' and I said to him, 'You don't get to sit there and talk to me about wrongdoing, you, the one who let time fuck him up the ass royally—you don't get to sit there and look at me with that pitiful face looking like you the only NDN who ever been hurt.'" My dear momma, I wanted to say, when did you become an owl caged in on all sides? "Ain't fucking fair, Jon, ain't fucking fair at all."

Her body caved in on itself, but the veins in her arms rose up and showed the royal blue blood that beat and beat and beat inside her. "He never let me call no one, saying it ain't my business, telling me this his fight, that he know a thing or two about scrapping with death." I got up and wrapped my arms around her from behind. "And when he went I lost me, Jon, I lost me real good. Feels like I ain't got nobody left—why everyone gotta leave me here to rot in this fucking hellhole, Jon?"

"You got me," I said. "And I'm not ever leaving, Momma." I rested my chin on her shoulder and we both stared into the distant corner of our kitchen. "Remember when you told me that neither of us weren't ever supposed to survive birth?" I said. She nodded and grasped my arm. "You told me, 'Jon, you, your Momma, we ain't the lie down and die type, we're survivors. That c-section or that pneumonia ain't take me and it sure as hell couldn't take you. The doctors said we had a week max and then come two, three, a month, a year, and then now, and you sure as hell better believe tomorrow.' You remember that, Momma? You told me, 'Never forget you born of Grandmother Earth, boy, you, the one who made me crave mud all the while I was pregnant with you.' And I picture you sometimes, Momma, sitting out there in the bush, dress soiled, all that dirt painting your fingers black, and you there, hair in a glorious braid running down your back, digging your hands into that dark, brown flesh. Then you scoop out the guts of the earth and you swallow ceremoniously, that mud slopping down your mouth and chest. And you smiling, Momma, you happy as all hell there in the bush, with your belly full of kokum askiy. And I picture that earth wrapping itself around our umbilical cord, Kokum there kissing us in the bathwater of your womb."

Momma laid her head on the table and broke down, dissolving into a yelping cry. I pressed myself against her and cried into her hair.

"I remember, m'boy," she said. "I told you when you left that we hardened ourselves to the world back then, that old Grandmother Earth gifted us a shell by wrapping around the braid that maintains us. We both born from a wound."

We held each other for what seemed a lifetime after that. We were so fucking helpless in our nostalgia, both so heavy with our sadness. When you really let yourself feel, well, you end up scaring yourself from all the hurt and pain.

L

My mom had planned a combined feast to celebrate both my ko-kum's birthday and Roger's life. Together, my mom and I did each other's makeup, and I helped pick out her dress. She looked beauti-ful in her medicine wheel jewellery.

I admired the two of us in the mirror. "Damn, Mom, if we weren't going to a funeral we'd have all the boys," I joked. "We're serving fish!" My mom had given up trying to learn the weird phrases I brought home, so she just nodded in agreement and con-tinued applying her lipstick. We may have been the saddest duo in the world right then and there, but we were radiant in our own ways. I decided that if I was going to feel anything, I'd experience both the pain and the joy—I'd be sullen and sexy, I'd walk into St. Peter's and own those wooden floorboards, I'd show the kids how it's done with a strut as mean as Naomi's and a face as fierce as Ashley Callingbull's. Serving fish? Hell, I was serving pickerel on a platter.

"Your kokum loved you, y'know that, with all her heart," my mom said out of the blue.

"I know, Mom."

"No, she really loved you—I think she loved you more than she ever did me." She got right stoic. "I always been a rotten kid to her, always yelling at her, running away." I felt her pain, so I put my head down in her lap and stared up at her.

"How I got pregnant so young, y'know?" I thought about Tias

and Jordan, thought about all the babies who had been raised by babies themselves.

"Told her I hated her too much—and that woman would whip my ass, y'know? But I loved her too, heck, we'd sit in the kitchen and make fun of each other for hours, but it was nice. I'd tell her, 'Heck, ol' lady, you're old enough to be first in with the other elders,' and she'd give me a slap. I'd tell her, 'Look at yer ol' tits, they're lower than your knees.'" I thought of how my kokum used to tell people, "Ah, you're useless as tits on a bull," whenever someone annoyed her.

"And she'd tell me, 'Ah shaddup, I'm still young enough to give you a good lickin' and cough-laugh like an ol' raven." My mom looked down at me, her eyes the colour of rocks. "But boy did she make me laugh, ain't no one I ever let talk to me like that but your kokum, y'know? The only woman who could ever make your daddy cry." She slid her hand beneath my body, cupped me under the knees.

"That man, boy I adored that man, he was tough as a bear but turned to a goddamn puddle when he was around your kokum." She pulled me in, closer, harder, until I was resting against her soft breasts. "He'd buy her hundreds of dollars of groceries, nice things too, y'know? And I always thought, 'You ain't ever buy me anything nice like this.'" Before I knew it, she was cradling me in her arms like a babe, the crown of my skull resting on her shoulder.

"He ain't ever buy me nothing nice like that—why? When she died, I asked her to forgive me. Heck, yeah, I was a bad kid, but I loved that woman so much it came out like hate." She looked down at me. "How come everyone kept loving her first? She had all the love, and threw me scraps like a rez dog. I always thought you loved her more too, m'boy, I always thought you wanted her as a mom." She inhaled deeply and then let out every bit of breath that lingered in her lungs. "I always thought you wanted her over me, always thought I wasn't no good for a boy like you."

"To love me, Momma, Kokum had to love you, too," I said as I untangled myself from her.

My mom's eyes brimmed with tears. "You kill me, m'boy, you absolutely kill me."

And I thought: we're both killing each other, Momma—we're both dying to get it right. I gave her a peck on the lips. She looked me in the eye and all of a sudden let loose a horrendous wail—every bit of breath, stink, and smoke came rushing forth from her belly and spat into the air. When her sobs subsided, she took me into her arms again.

"Every time I left her house she told me, 'You take care of that boy, y'hear?' I tried, I really tried," she said.

"Momma, I'm alive because of you." In her embrace I felt like a kid again, felt like I had yet to grow into my self.

I was home now, I felt it in my bones.

LI

The day after the service, my mom and I watched *The Price is Right* as we rolled out slabs of bannock to fry. She also had a pot of hangover soup boiling on the stove and a pan of oil warming up. In the fridge, some jello was setting overtop a layer of graham crackers—and a tub of Cool Whip was ready to be smeared all over it.

As we cooked, we yelled at the TV, giving the contestants advice on bids for the Showcase Showdown.

My mom put a hand on my upper arm. "Heck, you're just getting buff, m'boy." I smiled and shadow-boxed her and she pretended to faint. "Looks like you're eating well out there in the city," she said, then giggled softly. "You've really grown up, eh?"

I shrugged. "I guess so."

"You seeing anyone?"

"Not really."

"I know you ain't ever gonna bless me with no grandbabies and I'm fine with that. But it ain't right to be spending all this time by yourself, m'boy. You gotta find yourself a rock, ain't I tell you?"

"And a whole lotta medicine," I said, half-laughing.

She smiled. "You're really something, you know that?"

My mother's curls fell in front of her face and in the sunlight she looked as young as me.

"You should come visit me sometime in the city," I said.

"Yeah, I'll have to. Heck, them city boys probably ain't ready for me, babe. I'm still a sexy lady, annit?"

"You're still one hot tamale, Momma bear."

"Ain't that the truth?"

I tucked a curl behind her ear and she pulled me in for a hug. But it didn't feel like the others; it was softer, maybe sadder.

"What's wrong, Momma?" I asked.

"There won't be many more of these," she said. "There won't be many more moments like this, will there?"

We held each other. My beautiful mother, the best person I knew in this world, was crumbling beneath my weight and I couldn't help her—all I could do was hold onto her, lovingly, steadily.

"We got right now," I said.

And I thought about now, thought about my mom's advice: if I want to survive, I'd have to leave. But it's hard, you know? Each second I'm away from home is time that's gone forever, driving us that much closer to the end. How much more time do we really have? And by whose measure? Like she said, maybe there aren't that many more moments to come. But at least there was this one.

"I had this dream about you one night, y'know?" my mom said as she pulled me toward the couch where we sat down. "After your kokum died. That woman, always having her own crazy-ass dreams, but she told me I'd have one about you one day. Told me I had to tell you about it when I did. We're standing on this riverbed, you and me, and it's lined with all these big-ass Native men in regalia. They're spearfishing in this murky river. You and I move closer, but the men won't let me come with you, tell me it's a space reserved only for men, and then they stop you too when you move even closer. 'Only for men,' they repeat. From where we're standing, we can see the salmon swimming upstream—all these fish glittering like comets in the water. But none of the men can catch a single damn fish and you and I just start laughing at them. Then one of them comes up, in this heavy war paint, and he says, 'You think this funny, you try then, it ain't easy,' and he hands you this dinky little spear. You pick it up and move to the edge of the bank, cold water splashing on your bare legs, giving you goose bumps on your calves. They all laughing at you, call you girlboy. And I'm telling you to just let it go, that you ain't gotta prove nothing to no one. But you shake your head and walk deeper into the water and I can see those fish slapping you with their gills and tails. And then you ready your spear like you been doing this a hundred years and jab it into the water; when you pull it up, this big-ass fish is stuck to it. And all those men gasp and the women cheer because they hungry as all hell.

"Then you turn around to all of us, that fucking smirk of yours, sassy as ever, and I laugh and tell those men, 'That's my boy right there, that's my goddamn boy!' and you throw that fish on the ground, and the men are all just fucking right out of their minds. You go straight up to them as they gather around that damn fish and say, 'See, I ain't only a gatherer, I'm a hunter too!' and we all laugh this laugh that scares the birds right out the trees. And the men follow you back into the water, but you say, 'Patience,' and make them all stand there in the freezing cold, make them wait a goddamn century, until finally you nod and they all start jabbing their spears into the water, until they've all caught a fish themselves. And everybody cheers, bellies rumbling like thunder. And I see your kokum there in the middle of all those women, chortling. And she smiles and bobs her head like a little needle. She walks up to me and says, 'That boy of yours, Karen, he is his own best thing.' And I'm crying and saying, 'Momma, I'm so sorry,' and she says to me, she says, 'Me too baby, me too, but you're here, Karen, you're finally here.'" She wakes from retelling her dream and looks at me. "But you—you my everything, m'boy, all this time you been my rock."

"No, Momma," I replied, "you're my rock. I'm just the one who broke you."

"Maybe," she said, biting her lip. "But then you also the one who ground me. Ground me up into a medicine."

LII

I remember the first time Tias told me he loved me, all I could say in response was "Aw, ay-hay"—"thank you." His sheets had lost their grip from the corners of his mattress and were twisted around our thighs. His back was mucked with sweat and love juice, it felt like the marshlands at Oak Hammock. The bone spur in his shoulder was poking out as he raised himself off me and held my legs against his chest— bone so sharp, it looked as if it might pierce through his flesh. It was when he came that he said, "I love you." I didn't—couldn't—respond. Kokum always said that saying kisâkihitin was a summoning of a living being and Manito knows I ain't fit to be no mother. Plus what the hell did that even feel like, love? I'm not sure if I will ever feel it. I just know that when Tias leaves to go back to Jordan I will feel that pang in my belly, a pang that just sits there, heavy, hurting, whittling down as slowly as a cigarette. We lay in his bed for a while, me telling him about a new convenience store I found down on Osborne that sells cigarettes dirt cheap. He was listening as he always did, quietly, while I laid my head on his chest, his rib cage about as comfortable as a pile of remotes—Tias, always trying to be the stoic NDN.

My eyes fell on a photo of his sister on a table across from the bed—the sister he lost. "Hey Tee, tell me more about your sister," I said. "If you're up to it."

I could feel his steadiness break right away. He sat up, the sheets sheathed around him like he was some aerial silk dancer. It was a thorny subject; the story of his sister was buried deep within him, beneath a layer of sediment that had hardened into a gallstone, all cholesterol and jagged pain. It was then I decided that love sounded more like a full stop than a semi-colon, and I moved too much like water.

"'They took her away that day in that white car,'" he said, his body wilted like a deflated balloon. "Took me too, in spirit anyway. You think you know what loneliness feels like, Jon?" I wanted to say, yeah I think so, when I'm feeling alone, sometimes I down a beer and conjure up ghosts to keep me company because they ain't running up your monthly minutes. "I can't even begin to tell you how many times I dreamed of her, how many times I could still feel her tiny fist into my hand, my parents used to say they saved me from myself, you know? Like my real family ain't ever been fit to keep me. It's just, you ever feel—" His voice was low in his throat, so low that it faded into the air as soon as it came out of his mouth, so that only the dead could hear him speak. "You ever feel—like you ain't even here anymore?" I lit a cigarette and positioned myself behind him, cradling him with my legs, holding the cigarette in front of his lips so he could take a drag. "Like you're just shambling through the days, repeating what you've already done?" he continued. "Like life is all a blur and a ball of iron?" I placed my ear against his back, fitting into the groove of his spine, his heart pumping adrenaline and memory. His heartbeat was fierce, like a beaver slapping its tail.

"I can feel her, you know, tucked away behind the little pear sac in my stomach, like a goddamn fruit bowl that's gone moldy. And I'm sure there are bugs that eat from it too, I know, I see them cling to each other in a pile when I throw up after a rager. And when I go out and look at all these people smiling, shopping, holding their goddamn kid's hands in parks, I wonder if they feel this too. Or did I just inherit this from my dad who drank until his throat rotted and then gave up, said 'Fuck the air that I breathe, I'm gonna breathe in the dirt'?" Tias could nurse his hurt like it was the most precious baby in the world, but he fed it too much, birthed it into toilets and spewed it into the streets. He was a poet when he was sad, I thought—all those words, sharp like calligraphy.

He got up and went over to the picture of his sister, flecks of ash falling from his burning skin. He picked it up and stared at it. "I feel like I'm a goddamn prisoner sometimes, like I been locked away all my life while she's out there growing up and living her life without me," he said, rubbing his eyes. "And I don't even know if my baby sister is still alive." There he was, the boy beneath the surface, the one I loved who hid himself beneath sand and ash and all kinds of dead stories. Tias was woven like a spider web, all curious, all tangled, all sticky in corners but dazzling in the centre where the light shone through and coalesced around every cranny. My sad boy, lover, all sullen and defeated, the charm utterly broken, afraid, dead cold and stern as all hell like that old painter we studied, Waterhouse.

He looked at me. "You think she ever thinks about me, Jon? You think she ever stops and says, 'I wish my brother were here?'" I nod-ded, silent. This type of hurt was not mine to know—but then again, it was.

"I do," I finally replied. "I know it."

"How you know for sure?"

I pulled him back into the bed, lay his head in my lap. He could talk himself to death, that boy. I pricked my fingers as they grazed the sides of his head where his hair was buzzed, then ran them over to the top where his hair clumped together in dirty curls; I pulled it straight, the loose hairs shaking like a pine tree in a spring windstorm. I thought, *This here is how I know we're still alive, Tee—there's a whole world growing on top of your old head*, but he had fallen asleep by then.

"I know, m'boy, because you're the best damn person I ever met," I said, if only to myself.

LIII

Kokum had this wattle that made her look like a rooster decorated with a pearl necklace. When I was a kid, she'd sit me on her knee and let me pick from one of two cookie tins she kept on her table. She was a tricky woman and would fill one with gingersnaps and the other with her sewing materials—she took too much from Bob Barker, thinking all things had to be a damn gamble. On her lap I'd play with her wattle and she'd fill her kitchen with that deep throaty bingo-hall laugh all Cree women seem to have inherited—a sound so bellowing that you wonder how such a little woman could make such loud sounds from deep inside her belly. When she was older, I'd lay in her lap and look up at her dark, prune-like eyes that caught the light in each of their folds.

At her funeral, where I was a pallbearer, I learned her middle name was Maude: Frances Maude Sutherland. It felt like such a foreign language to call her anything but Kokum. All those syllables heavy as all hell on the tongue, but my kokum was as light as air and as fierce as the rapids in her backyard. The church was afloat from the voices of all her kin singing gospels—a harmony of NDN voices orating about an old rugged cross and emblems of suffering and shame and crowns and blood. And it was funny, you know, my kokum, even in a casket made of oak and filled with sweet grass, still felt light even for my femme-boy arms—but even still, my arms shook like leaves.

I never did make it back to the rez to hear that story from Kokum, the story of who I am. She saved it for me after I left, and I never made it back in time. After some of my cousins turned their backs on me out there, said if I ever returned to the rez they'd beat my ass, I really had no desire to return, especially without Jordan and Tias there. I wanted so much to hate Roger who thought like them, and hate my mom for loving him, and hate the home that squeezed the queer right out of its languages. I think about my kokum a lot now, I wonder what she would have told me, if she would've brought out that old sewing kit and made me a pair of slippers and said, "Just watch." What would she have said to me, the boy she raised and whose diapers she changed, the boy she bathed and kissed and taught all about porcupines and other sharp objects—what would she have said if she'd known I got naked on webcams and rubbed myself raw for a few measly ass bucks?

"Moving south," she hummed when I told her I was leaving, "gonna be cold, take these slippers, m'boy." She handed me a pair, hand-knitted, green as the spikes of the evergreens mixed with wolf-grey. Those slippers are still in my closet, and I think about all the folds, those colours, the way she'd weave a hole big enough for your feet, all of this, accomplished little by little. I think about what all went into those slippers, all those wishful thoughts, those hands that smelled of bannock and tea, NCI-FM playing Loretta Lynn in between bouts of the entire rez wishing so-and-so a happy birthday during commercial breaks. I think of the skin and dirt and grit that's stained deep into the grains of that fibre from her nail beds, the scent of her perfume, her tears, blood, saliva, cells, her stories, all of her wrapped up in the weave of her knitting. "You know, they say south is the direction of youth, the time of summer, healing, coming in, direction of the body, m'boy. You gonna be changing, and that's fine, but you come back when you do, okay? You come back here and you change me, too." We pinky swore and giggled like children, that smile of hers making me feel alive.

At the celebratory feast for Kokum, we all sat at her table passing bowls of gravy and plates of bannock and stew. Even the Chief showed up, along with the neighbours, all my cousins, Momma, Roger, my uncles and aunties—seemed the whole damn rez was cooped up in that little three-bedroom house that let hot winds blow through it like an open field. After our meal, all us NDNs sat cross-legged on the floor, looking like kids again, the WWE playing on the TV in homage to Kokum. We told stories and laughed, which may sound like a weird thing to do after the death of the matriarch who held us all together like a glue that couldn't quit. These days, I hear the house is empty mostly; we never get those same reunions save for Mother's Day and her birthday. Big old haunted house planted there in the middle of the rez, windows lined with dust, lights stained that old yellow hue, thin filaments on their last legs, everything screaming: witness me.

"You know, nimama, she caught me one time with your poppa," my mom said, "right there in front of the house, both just right snapped and making out like sloppy old fish in the backseat of her old beat-up wagon. She flashed the porch lights on and off to break us up and gave me the lickin of a lifetime when I finally came in, tail between my legs like a damn rez pup. I tell ya, that wooden spoon was bound to break in half whipping against my ass—but that's just the type of person your kokum was, stiff as a goddamn board that never quit, for fuck sakes, we still even cook with that old spoon." And the room erupted in more laughter as we passed around stories like cigarettes. One of my aunties chirped in, "Your poppa told me she came out onto that porch damn near bare ass with that spoon in hand chasing him off down into the bush, told him, 'Boy you better git, come around here sloppy as that kissing my girl right in front of my home, will ya?'" And I swear you never heard a room laugh so hard, everyone turning into stand-up comedians all of a sudden. One of my uncles jumped in. "Heard that next time your pops called she told him, 'Your woman's gone off to the pow wow with a real dancer, ain't no swindling pig like your slack ass,'" he said, half with burps and half in that rez slang that made their speech sound as fast as the four-wheeler ripping through the hunting ground. "Then your old pops comes around, sad as all hell, with this right slack apple pie he picked up at Hodgsons and tried to pass off as homemade like Mrs. Doubtfire or something."

Momma was in that mode of laughing where she had to slap everything around her and throw her head back like it was about to roll off. "Kokum ate his pie and put him straight to work," she said. "Made him cut the whole damn yard with a push-mower while all those rez dogs nipped at him. I die laughing every time he used to tell me how he had to cut the entire rez's grass and kick at dogs that'd pounce up on his leg and just give'r on his legs. Don't have a clue in holy hell how that woman knew, knew that my belly had you growing up in it. She beat time into our asses, whooped us up into real NDNs.

And then your pops, he goes up to her one day, says, 'Hey Frances,' and you could see her veins just rise on her neck because everyone knows you only called her Momma or Kokum, and he says, 'Can you like, you know, do it when you pregnant? I mean like, do you gotta be abstinent and all that for nine months cause it ain't safe?' And Momma, she calls me into the room, says, 'Karen, you hear this boy? He thinks he's Long John Silver,' and we both laughed hard enough to get abs. 'Boy,' she says, 'you ain't gonna hurt no one with that little pecker of yours.'"

Today, Kokum is beneath a stone marker that says, "In our hearts you will live forever," in a rickety cemetery overfilled with NDN people. I sit down cross-legged in front of her, feel the flattened prick of new grass poking into my calves, that fresh smell of severed blades and growth all trying to mask the smell of trauma that always seems to permeate graveyards. The heat is beating down on me and my black T-shirt is soaking it all up, so I take it off, tuck it into my back pocket. Bare-chested, I wrap my legs around her tombstone, hold on tightly with my arms wrapped around its tip.

I want to tell you so many things Kokum, tell you, I think I made it, you know, travelled south and survived. I want to say, I just hope I ain't changed too much, y'know, hell, I hope I ain't changed into no emblem of shame. And I know what you gonna say to me, you're gonna say humility, m'boy, sacred teaching, don't you know? And I'll say what humility got to do with shame? And you'll say humility is just a humiliation you loved so much it transformed. And I'll say, what the heck does that mean? And you'll say, boy, you ever swear at me again and I'll give you a smack upside that bean-shaped head of yours. Just look at these hands, you'll say. I'd look at them and see palms full of raggedness, lines intersecting every which way, cup of cosmos, bowl of infinite. Just watch, you'll tell me, just keep on watching.

I watched too much, Kokum, watched your body disintegrate back into a root, watched your breath expunge and that little line flatten, watched them all discuss how "pulling the plug" was the only gift we had left to give. The hell is left to watch, Kokum? I tighten my body around her, will myself to stone. *Why you ain't take me with you? You said you'd never leave me be, why'd you make me promise you to come back changed if you're gonna leave me before I do? Why'd you let me leave, Kokum? Why'd you never get that wooden spoon and say, "Boy, get your ass home and visit me right now"? Why'd you let time whittle you to sand before you ask me home?*

Then I let loose a scream that threw those crows back into the sky, and pounded my fist into the ground over and over, cutting my knuckles. I bleed into the earth beside her. *Who the hell gonna love me now, Kokum? Whose gonna suck the pain from my skin, teach me to love it into humility? Who, Kokum, who?*

I cry myself into a stupor, lungs inhaling staccato breaths, and I lie there until the sun sweeps across the sky, less a beating heat, more a red morphing into pink, kissing the blue of the night pouring in on the horizon. *Hey Kokum? I'm sorry, you know, I never meant to hurt you. I never meant to forget those weekend calls and visit even less; never meant to be drunk the last time I said I loved you before you got sick and couldn't talk. I never got to say thank you for all those stories*

you gave me that filled my belly. I'm sorry I let home become this: a
stone and fields of grass and a tree. And I'm sorry, Kokum, I'm sorry I
never got to show you how I transform.

There's snot and tears on her headstone, which I wipe delicately
with my T-shirt. I kiss her name and promise I'll come back, this time
for real. I will a smile and head back towards home, Momma is sure
to be wondering where the heck I am by now. I walk down the gravel
road, heading west, my shirt in my hand. The rez is quiet tonight save
for the crickets chirping lullabies in the bush around us; the setting
sun is a kaleidoscope now—every colour crackling around its edges.
The light dances on me, I can feel its dim heat swirl down my spine
and settle into the rivulet on my lower back, it pools itself there while
the new cold of the west makes my nipples harden into points. I look
back at how far I've walked since I left Kokum, a couple of solid ki-
lometres, my shadow now stretching across the road. And then I see
it in the elongated shadows barreling from the east: a hunched woman holding my hand made from that illusive prism sky. When I look
down at my hand, I see only my T-shirt there—a shirt full of dried
sweat and blood and phlegm.

Maybe that's why the only bit of me I left was a ghost? I guess
that's all we left each other, eh Kokum, just each other's spirits? One
for you, one for Momma too—maybe that's why Manito gifted me
two? Manito gifted me enough to travel out and in and all that space
between, to weave like those old rapids do, and to carry memories as
a souvenir between this world and the fourth, where I'll finally come
home and have nothing but my glories to share with you.

LIV

The only time an NDN pulls out their own photo album is when someone dies. My dad is in ours, so is my kokum and Mush and Roderick—and now, so was Roger. Whenever we used to bring it out, my aunties and uncles all gathered around and talked stories. The album was our allowance to remember. Everyone came to see the photos with bannock and stew and dried meat in hand. We ate, we drank, we laughed and cried in unison. My kokum had a story for every photo; stories that redeemed even the alcoholics and the baby daddies, stories that love and scream in pain in equal measure. It's all there; we're all there. But here, now, it's just us two. And there are blank pages for my mom and me.

When I look back at these old photos, I see my family come alive; I see their youth, but I also see them aging and dying and living their lives. It's overwhelming to think about all the stories that we've made, helped to tell, helped to create—our bodies are a library, and our stories are written like braille on the skin. I wouldn't trade it for the world; I love the noise, the liveliness of voices that are laughing, arguing, bingo-calling, and telling stories in a too-packed home. In fact, I'd say, that's my world.

We're all here telling our stories in NDN time.

But the ironic thing I've learned about NDN time is that it's an elixir of an excuse and a toxin of a measurement.

It'll kill you, you know, if you love it too dearly.

And that's the truth.

kinanâskomitin

I write this book with the goal of showing you that Two-Spirit and queer Indigenous folx are not a "was," that we are not the ethnographic and romanticized notations of "revered mystic" or "shamanic," instead we are an *is* and a *coming*. In nehiyawewin, there are no masculine or feminine attributes, instead we have animations in which we hold all our relations. We are accountable to those kin, be they inanimate or non-human, or be they unabashedly queer, femme, bottom, pained, broken. We put our must vulnerable in the centre and for once I do just that: 2S folx and Indigenous women are centred here. I hold our relations accountable to us for once. Jonny has taught me a lot of things but there are two that I want to share with you: one, a good story is always a healing ceremony, we recuperate, re-member, and rejuvenate those we storytell into the world; and two, if we animate our pain, it becomes something we can make love to.

I need to thank all of the Two-Spirit, queer, trans, and non-binary folks and allies who have paved the way for me to write a book like this: Gwen Benaway, Billy-Ray Belcourt, Tommy Pico, Qwo-Li Driskill, Tomson Highway, Sharron Proulx-Turner, Ma-Nee Chacaby, Beverly Little Thunder, Daniel Heath Justice, Arielle Twist, Chrystos, Deborah Miranda, Gregory Scofield, M. Carmen Lane, Beth Brant, Janice Gould, Aiyyana Maracle, Lee Maracle, Leanne Betasamosake Simpson, Chelsea Vowel, Chip Livingston, Natalie Diaz, and so many others I hold near and dear to my heart. I also want to give a big thank-you, ay-hay, to Cherie Dimaline for showing me that 2S folx can survive and thrive in the apocalypse; Eden Robinson for gifting us with her lovingly pained narrator, Jared; Richard Van Camp for orating Larry Sole into the world, and for guiding me powerfully throughout the writing of *Jonny*; and to Katherena Vermette for showing me the corners of Winnipeg that have always been heavy with hope.

Ay-hay to everyone who has helped with *Jonny Appleseed*'s creation, most importantly kise-manito. I need to thank Aritha van Herk and the entire class of the University of Calgary's ENGL 694, "One Hundred Pages in One Hundred Days" for all their guidance, mentorship, kindness, and fierce editorial feedback during the beginning stages of this novel: Richard Kemick, Marc Lynch, Michaela Stephen, Donna Williams, and others who helped me in that class. Thanks to Indigenous Arts and Stories for providing me with a one-week stay in the Banff Leighton Studios where I secluded myself to write in the mountains, putting out tobacco every morning for kise-manito, cried remembering too much, and listened to round dance music into the wee hours of the morning as I finished writing Jonny into the world. Thanks to *The Malahat Review* and *Prairie Fire* for publishing the earliest segments of this book. Thanks to Gwen Benaway and Brian Lam for your editorial help and empowering feedback. Thanks to Erin Konsmo for the gorgeous cover and working so closely with me during its inception. The work you do alongside NSYHN inspires me to no end. All love to my committee members, who I think of as dear friends and kin: Larissa Lai, Derritt Mason, and Rain Prud'homme-Cranford, who in their own way helped me find the words to write this novel. I owe a gigantic thank-you to Peguis First Nation, Treaty One, Selkirk,

Winnipeg, and all of manitowapow for always filling my belly with story. Thanks to Darin Flynn, Elder Elmer Morningchild (okimâw piyêsiw napêw), and Merion Hodgson for teaching me so much about nehiyawewin and speaking me back into my spirits. Thanks to Peter Bernt Hanson, nîcimos, for reading through this manuscript so many times and loving me all the more for it. Thanks to nikâwiy, Tina Whitehead, nîtisân, Krista Whitehead and Tyra Cameron, nistim, Akira Budge, nikâwîsak, Cecelia Stevenson, Terri Cameron, Lorraine Whitehead, Margaret Whitehead, and nohkômak, Beverly Cameron, Rose Whitehead, and Frances Sutherland: you are the avatars who animate Jonny, and I owe you everything. Thanks to nohtâwiy, Peter Whitehead, nîtisân, Cole Cameron and Quinn Budge, and all my cousins, who are really my brothers, Tim, Sidney (Chooch), Wallace (Pap), Tyler, who have allowed me to be as queer and as Indigenous as I damn well want to be throughout my life. And thank you to all the other strong, beautiful, and resilient Indigenous women, 2S, trans, queer, and non-binary folx in my life—this book is for you. Ay-hay, kisâkihitinawaw!

JOSHUA WHITEHEAD is an Oji-Cree/nehiyaw, Two-Spirit/ Indigiqueer member of Peguis First Nation (Treaty 1). He is the author of *full-metal indigiqueer* (Talonbooks, 2017) and the winner of the Governor General's History Award for the Indigenous Arts and Stories Challenge in 2016. Currently he is working on a PhD in Indigenous Literatures and Cultures in the University of Calgary's English department (Treaty 7). *Jonny Appleseed* is his first novel.